Dear Reader,

When I came up with the character of Shelby Jacobs, I envisioned her as the sidekick in my first Flipside novel. But it quickly became apparent that this woman was in control of the story. She's hip, sassy and not afraid to speak her mind.

Sure, her life might be a little out of control at the moment, but she's working on that. And she *knows* she's the bane of Dallas Williams's existence, but she figures that's *his* problem. She only gets in his way when it's absolutely necessary, and *she's* the one fighting their sexual fascination. He's perfectly willing to throw caution to the wind and complicate their lives unbearably.

I hope you enjoy Shelby's journey, from getting arrested to rescuing risqué photos to falling for the one man she needs to avoid. I had an absolutely delightful time writing her story, and I'm excited to share it.

If you'd care to drop me a line through my Web site at www.barbaradunlop.com, I'd love to hear from you.

Happy reading.

Barbara Dunlop

"What have you got on her?"

Dallas asked, turning to the uniformed officer.

The arresting officer opened his black notebook. "We have three hundred pirated copies of *Midnight Run*, two-dozen Uzis, ten AK-47s and a bazooka."

Shelby sucked in a quick breath. "I didn't—"

"As your attorney, I've advised you to keep your mouth shut."

Her eyes emitted more sapphire sparks. This time Dallas felt them for sure. Perfect. Sexual awareness. Perhaps one of the officers would be good enough to shoot him now.

"Name?" the desk sergeant repeated.

Shelby mutinously kept her mouth shut.

"You can answer *that*," said Dallas with a sigh.

"Why thank you. Shelby Jacobs. I didn't know about any of the guns. I've—"

"Just your name," interrupted Dallas.

She clamped her jaw shut again and muttered something between her clenched teeth. It was going to be a long night....

Barbara Dunlop
Out of Order

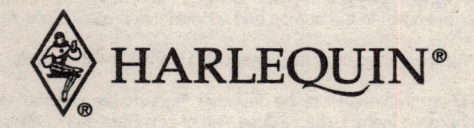

HARLEQUIN®

TORONTO • NEW YORK • LONDON
AMSTERDAM • PARIS • SYDNEY • HAMBURG
STOCKHOLM • ATHENS • TOKYO • MILAN • MADRID
PRAGUE • WARSAW • BUDAPEST • AUCKLAND

If you purchased this book without a cover you should be aware that this book is stolen property. It was reported as "unsold and destroyed" to the publisher, and neither the author nor the publisher has received any payment for this "stripped book."

ISBN 0-373-44196-7

OUT OF ORDER

Copyright © 2004 by Barbara Dunlop.

All rights reserved. Except for use in any review, the reproduction or utilization of this work in whole or in part in any form by any electronic, mechanical or other means, now known or hereafter invented, including xerography, photocopying and recording, or in any information storage or retrieval system, is forbidden without the written permission of the publisher, Harlequin Enterprises Limited, 225 Duncan Mill Road, Don Mills, Ontario, Canada M3B 3K9.

All characters in this book have no existence outside the imagination of the author and have no relation whatsoever to anyone bearing the same name or names. They are not even distantly inspired by any individual known or unknown to the author, and all incidents are pure invention.

This edition published by arrangement with Harlequin Books S.A.

® and TM are trademarks of the publisher. Trademarks indicated with ® are registered in the United States Patent and Trademark Office, the Canadian Trade Marks Office and in other countries.

www.eHarlequin.com

Printed in U.S.A.

ABOUT THE AUTHOR

Flipside author Barbara Dunlop writes romantic comedy stories curled up in a log cabin in Canada's far north, where bears outnumber people and it snows six months of the year. Fortunately, she has a brawny husband and two teenage children to haul firewood, feed the horses and plow the driveway while she sips cocoa and muses about her upcoming chapters.

A two-time winner of the RWA Golden Heart Award, Barbara has written for the Temptation, Duets and Flipside lines for Harlequin. She loves to travel to writers' conferences to meet fellow authors and explore new cities—though reporting the first leg of the journey by dogsled can sometimes be exhausting.

Barbara loves to hear from readers in big cities and small towns all over the world. You can contact her through her Web site at www.barbaradunlop.com.

Books by Barbara Dunlop

HARLEQUIN DUETS
54B—THE MOUNTIE STEALS A WIFE
90B—A GROOM IN HER STOCKING
98A—THE WISH-LIST WIFE

HARLEQUIN TEMPTATION
848—FOREVER JAKE
901—NEXT TO NOTHING!
940—TOO CLOSE TO CALL

Don't miss any of our special offers. Write to us at the following address for information on our newest releases.

Harlequin Reader Service
U.S.: 3010 Walden Ave., P.O. Box 1325, Buffalo, NY 14269
Canadian: P.O. Box 609, Fort Erie, Ont. L2A 5X3

For my son, Eric

1

WHEN THE COP burst through the front door of Gerry's Game-O-Rama video arcade with his gun drawn and his eyes suspicious slits in a pug-dog face, Shelby Jacobs should have guessed her day was headed straight downhill.

His partner whipped around the steel-bar reinforced door and Shelby took a startled step away from the cash register, subconsciously getting ready to duck if the bullets started flying.

She'd known when she'd taken this job last week that Black Street wasn't in the best part of Chicago. But it was the first one she'd been offered. It was near the El Station and only fifteen minutes from her friend Allison's apartment.

And beggars, as they said, couldn't be choosers.

"Nobody move," shouted the pug-dog cop as he hustled between video terminal number six and the Rally Car Challenge, twisting his gun from side to side to keep everybody in his sights. His holster hit a half-empty bag of popcorn, scattering white kernels across the black strip of rubber that disguised a cracked concrete floor.

Cop number two held his position, gun at the ready, eyes scanning the crowd of a dozen or so streetwise teenagers, all but daring somebody to make a sudden move. The gamers's hands stilled on the controls and the pings and simulated tire squeals died away.

Shelby found it a little hard to believe that desperate criminals would drop in for a round of Midnight Run between heists. But, what did she know? Once you'd robbed the bank, she supposed you had the rest of the day to kill.

Squat and broad-shouldered, his divided chin tipped at an arrogant angle, the pug-dog cop came to a halt in front of Shelby.

Her hand reflexively tightened around a fistful of game tokens as her stomach clenched to the size of a walnut.

He tipped slightly forward, his unibrow dropping even lower over his dark eyes. "I'm lookin' for Gerry Bonnaducci."

The unexpected statement surprised the fear right out of her. "You want *Gerry*?"

"Where is he?"

"What did he do?" Gerry had been right here since ten o'clock this morning. Shelby could vouch for that.

"Put your hands on the counter." Pug-dog's voice lowered to a growl as he trained his gun on her.

Staring down the steel-gray muzzle of his .38 was definitely enough to convince Shelby to give up Gerry. Employee loyalty only went so far.

"He's in the back," she said.

"Put your hands on the counter where I can see them"

"But—"

"Now!"

Right. Shelby slapped her palms against the faded,

gray Formica countertop, crunching the metal tokens against her palm.

A muscle in the cop's cheek twitched and he shifted his gun, barrel pointing to the ceiling. He nodded to his partner, who nodded back and fixed his attention on Shelby.

Then pug-dog crept along the counter toward the office where Gerry was feeding coins into the separating machine. The sound of quarters, dimes and nickels clanked and clattered through the closed door, counterpoint to the repetitive rap music and synthesized voices patiently giving next instructions to the frozen players.

Shelby wondered if she should give the players refunds for their interrupted games. Gerry was a bit of a tightwad, but surely under these circumstances they deserved a replay.

Pug-dog kicked the office door open with his black boot.

"Freeze," he yelled, planting his feet apart, both hands training the gun on Gerry.

Gerry swiveled in his seat. His eyes widened, and the cigar dropped out of his mouth, knocking once against his striped tie before hitting the concrete floor, leaving an ash trail as it rolled to a stop.

He didn't protest or ask any questions while pug-dog slapped the cuffs on his chubby wrists and began reciting his Miranda rights. He looked for all the world like he'd done this before.

Great. Now she was working for a criminal. What was with her? Did she have a *bad-boss* magnet stuck to her forehead?

Last week, her cheating, scumbag boyfriend had fired her from the Terra Suma Cocktail Lounge in Minneapolis. That time she'd lost her job, her home, her boyfriend and her future all in one fell swoop.

At least she hadn't been sleeping with Gerry. Thank goodness for small favors.

Really small favors.

She was jobless again. And who knew when or *if* she'd get a paycheck for this week's work.

This did it. She was getting a real job next time. Even if it meant college courses at night. Even if it meant, Lord help her, moving back in with her parents.

She never should have dropped out of philosophy in third year. Come to think of it, she never should have taken philosophy in the first place. She should have taken accounting or business management or nursing. Something with a future—

"Hands behind your back, ma'am."

Shelby turned to see cop number two circling around the end of the sales counter.

"But—"

"Behind your back, ma'am." He was taller than his partner, younger, with dark, wavy hair and brown eyes. He strode toward her, his broad chest a wall of silver badge and imposing navy-blue uniform.

"Why?" It was more a squeak than a question as she tipped up her chin to maintain eye contact.

"You're under arrest on suspicion of selling pirated software and prohibited firearms." He unclipped the handcuffs from the back of his utility belt.

Shelby stared at the dangling steel bracelets in morbid fascination. "Firearms?"

"Hands behind your back, ma'am." The cop latched onto her nerveless wrist, twisting it neatly into the small of her spine.

"But I didn't... I'm not..."

"You can tell it all to the judge."

"The *judge?*" A series of rapid clicks echoed in her ears as the cold cuffs clapped tightly around her wrists.

"Gerry," she called, trying not to let panic collapse what was left of her stomach. "Tell them I had nothing to do with this."

"Nothing to do with *what?*" asked Gerry as pug-dog steered him toward the exit. He shook his head in apparent disgust. "It's a bogus bust."

"The detectives are out back searching your warehouse right now," said pug-dog, shooing the twelve teenagers out of the Game-O-Rama in front of him.

"But, I'm *innocent.*" Shelby couldn't get arrested. It was nearly four-thirty, and Allison was expecting her. They were going dancing at Balley's tonight.

She'd hauled herself out of bed early this morning to drop her emerald dress off at the Flower-Fresh Drycleaner's. Which, by the way, closed in half an hour.

"So am I," called Gerry.

The second cop clapped his hand on Shelby's shoulder, and she felt a renewed jolt of panic as he urged her into a walk.

"Don't you need evidence or something?" she asked, mind racing for a way out of the predicament. She wasn't a criminal. She was a cashier, a cocktail waitress. Sure, maybe she didn't have the best judgment in the world, particularly when it came to men, but that was hardly a crime.

His look was grim, all business. "We have some pretty compelling evidence."

"On me?"

"On you."

"That's impossible."

"Did you or did you not make a pickup in the company van at Michigan and Eighteenth yesterday afternoon?"

Shelby searched her memory as they cleared the counter and headed for the door. "That was coffee."

The cop rolled his eyes. "Two hundred-pound crates of *coffee*?"

"Two sixteen-ounce *cups* of coffee."

"I'm talking about the merchandise they loaded in the back."

"Who loaded? What back?"

"The two crates of Uzis. Surely you remember that little detail. We have it all on videotape."

Uzis? Shelby blinked. *"Uzis?"*

"Yes, ma'am."

She'd been inside the coffee shop all of three minutes. "How can that be? It was coffee. I bought *coffee*."

The cop pushed the door open in front of her, and car horns and engine revs overtook the beeps of the computer terminals. "That's your story, and you're stickin' to it?"

An exhaust-filled breeze hit her square in the face. "It's the truth."

"Right," he drawled. "The Uzis in your warehouse tell a different story."

"I didn't even know we *had* a warehouse. And I've never seen an Uzi. Well, except on television. And that one time at the airport in Brazil. I'm an innocent bystander."

"I believe the technical term is 'accomplice.'"

"This is outrageous," Shelby protested, anger asserting itself over her confusion.

But then they crossed the sidewalk, and her momentary bravado disappeared. She cringed, suddenly conscious of the drivers and pedestrians passing by on the busy street. Not that she'd ever see them again. And not that she was the first person to be arrested on Black Street.

Still...

"You can tell it all to the judge when we get downtown," said the cop.

Shelby felt the first ray of hope. "You mean, right away? Like tonight?" The judge would *have* to believe she was innocent. Maybe he'd free her before Allison could worry. And then her life could carry on as normal—such as normal was this month.

"Could we stop at Flower-Fresh on the way to the station?" she asked.

"No."

"But, my dress—" She caught the look in his eyes and snapped her mouth shut.

"You won't need a dress where you're going."

Shelby swallowed, gaze sliding away from his, her optimism bottoming out. "You mean, the station house, right?"

"I meant the lockup."

"They might put me in jail?"

"That's the usual procedure."

"But, I didn't *do* anything."

The cop reached down to open the back door of his cruiser. "That's what they all say."

"Don't I get a telephone call?" Allison's new fiancé was a lawyer. Maybe Greg could rescue her.

"Not yet. Watch your head."

Staring into the murky, pungent depths of the

cruiser's back seat, Shelby's entire body recoiled in a wave of instant claustrophobia. She had to fight an urge to kick the cop in the shin and make a run for it.

She was going to Balley's tonight—to drink shooters and laugh with Allison about rotten, cheating boyfriends and their nasty blond floozies. She wasn't going to get strip-searched, eat gruel and sleep on a lumpy prison mattress with a woman named Spike.

But the cop was a whole lot bigger and stronger than she was. He planted her firmly on the bench seat.

"There's been a mistake," she whispered.

"Then you have nothing to worry about." He slammed the handleless door shut and headed around the hood of the car.

Shelby hated to disagree with the nice policeman, but she had plenty to worry about. The cops didn't believe she was innocent. Gerry wasn't going to help her. And they had her on videotape making an Uzi pickup at a coffee shop cum firearms depot.

Her shoulders slumped and she let her head drop back against the hard seat, closing her eyes in defeat.

Gunrunner was going to look even worse than philosophy major on her résumé.

IF HONOR and principles weren't already keeping lawyer Dallas Williams on the straight and narrow, the thought of spending more than ten minutes in the Haines Street lockup certainly would.

It had to be one of the most depressing places on earth. Fluorescent overheads buzzed and flickered against faded, gray ceilings. Prisoners shouted profanity from the long lockup hallway behind the desk sergeant's counter. And the smell of mildew permeated the punky, dark walnut paneling, circa 1930.

"Got that arrest report ready for Dallas Williams?" the desk sergeant called to the officer behind him as two uniforms brought a man and a woman to the desk for processing.

Dallas automatically shifted away from the handcuffed female. He was here to get background information on a witness in an embezzlement hearing, and then he was out of here.

"Be about two minutes," the sergeant called to Dallas. He gestured to the royal-blue, molded plastic chairs that lined the opposite side of the hallway. "Want to have a seat?"

Dallas shook his head. "No thanks."

Rule number one in the Haines Street lockup was to stay well away from both the furniture and the clientele. He didn't need gum stuck to the backside of his Armani's. And he had no desire to chat with the colorful southside characters camped out, waiting for friends and relatives to post bail.

He felt the female prisoner staring up at him and glanced down to meet green eyes that were surprisingly clear and lucid.

"Are you Dallas *Williams?*" she asked.

She was five-foot-six, with wavy auburn hair that just brushed her tanned shoulders. She was too fresh-faced to be a Lakeshore Drive hooker, but that black tank top and the tight miniskirt gave him pause. She was willowy thin, and he was sure she wasn't nearly dangerous enough to warrant the cuffs.

"Of Turnball, Williams and Smith?" she continued when he didn't answer.

"I am," he acknowledged with a cautious nod.

She smiled, tipping her head to one side, revealing white teeth that had probably cost her parents a fortune. She looked instantly relieved, as if he'd just admitted to being her guardian angel. "Thank goodness. I was going to try calling Greg, but this is even better."

The desk sergeant pushed a manila envelope across the scarred countertop. "Here's your report, Mr. Williams."

"Thanks." Dallas picked up the police report and started past her for the door. Last thing he needed was to let this woman pour out her soul.

"Wait," angel-eyes called, lurching toward him before the arresting officer grabbed her firmly by the elbow and yanked her back.

Focusing on her hairline, and ignoring a jolt of hostility toward the officer, Dallas gave her a polite nod of goodbye and kept moving.

"You have to help me," she cried.

Dallas shook his head, and fixed his focus on the exit door. Fresh-faced or not, he didn't represent hookers, drug addicts and petty southside criminals. Not now, not ever.

"Please," she implored, even louder.

Dallas stopped, gritted his teeth and pivoted to face her. "I charge three hundred dollars an hour."

She drew back in surprise, her eyes widening, their color seeming to lighten. Tank top and skirt not withstanding, she suddenly looked out of place in the harsh grunge of stained walls, scarred furnishings and world-weary cops. *"Really?"*

"Really," he answered. Not that her looks made one iota of difference. World-weary or not, the Haines

Street squad wasn't in the habit of bringing in innocent people.

They didn't need to. They had plenty of criminals to choose from.

"How fast do you think you could get me out of here? Ten? Fifteen minutes?"

"I have an eight-hour minimum on new cases," he lied.

She blinked, and this time her eyes looked turquoise.

"That can't be legal," she said.

"I assure you, it's perfectly legal. They make you study that sort of thing for the bar exam."

"Well it's definitely not moral."

"You want to debate morality? You're the criminal. I'm a law-abiding businessman."

"I'm not a criminal."

Dallas couldn't even believe he was having this conversation. Couldn't believe she had the audacity to take him on. Couldn't believe she was standing here in handcuffs, eyes shooting sapphire sparks at him for absolutely no reason.

"Pirated software and illegal firearms," said the arresting officer to the desk sergeant.

Dallas cocked his head sideways, raising his eyebrows at her. Part of him couldn't wait to see what she had to say about that.

"I was in the wrong job at the wrong time."

The uniformed cop beside her chuckled and shook his head. Like Dallas, he'd heard every excuse in the book. This one wasn't even particularly creative.

The woman shot the cop an annoyed glare before turning her attention back to Dallas. She squared her shoulders. "I'm innocent. And I'm Allison Kempler's roommate. If you won't help me, perhaps you'd be good enough to let Greg know I'm here."

At the mention of Allison's name, Dallas groaned inwardly. Leaving the woman here to be booked and locked up suddenly ceased to be an option. Greg was batty about his new fiancée. If Dallas upset Allison, there'd be hell to pay.

"Greg Smith," she elaborated. "Allison's fiancé."

"Name and address," said the sergeant.

"Son of a bitch," Dallas muttered under his breath, stuffing the envelope under his arm and taking two steps back to the counter. "What've you got on her?" he asked the arresting officer.

"I'm not paying you twenty-four-hundred dollars," she said.

"We'll talk about the bill later," he said.

"Oh, no, we won't. Do I look stupid?"

"No." Crazy, maybe. But definitely not stupid.

"You may think you've got me right where you want—"

"Shut up."

"Excuse me?"

Dallas turned and subjected her to a long, steady stare. It was unseemly to argue about fees in front of the police department. And, quite frankly, right where he wanted her wasn't in the Haines Street lockup.

It was...

He pulled his thoughts up short, clamping his jaw. Where the hell had that come from?

"We'll come to a *mutually* agreeable fee once I get you out of those cuffs," he said.

Her eyes narrowed. She nodded, but he could see it cost her a lot to keep her latest opinion to herself.

The arresting officer flipped open his black notebook. "We have three-hundred pirated copies of *Midnight Run*, two dozen Uzis, ten AK-47s and a bazooka. And we've got another warrant for the garage across the alley."

Shelby sucked in a quick breath. "I didn't—"

"As your attorney, I've advised you to keep your mouth shut."

Her eyes emitted some more sapphire sparks.

This time Dallas felt them all the way to his toes.

Perfect. Sexual awareness. Perhaps one of the officers would be good enough to shoot him now.

"Name?" the desk sergeant repeated.

Shelby mutinously kept her mouth shut.

"You can answer that," said Dallas with a sigh.

"Why, thank you. Shelby Jacobs. I didn't know about any of the guns. I've only been at Game-O-Rama for a week. Ask Allison—"

"Just your name," said Dallas.

She clamped her jaw shut again and muttered something between her clenched teeth. He was pretty sure it concerned his parentage.

Like *he* was the problem here.

"Anything connecting Ms. Jacobs directly to the evidence?" he asked.

"We have videotape of her making a pickup." The cop paused significantly. "She claims she thought it was coffee."

"I—"

Dallas rapped Shelby's ankle with the side of his foot. To his shock, she actually did shut up this time.

"Did you see her make a payment?" he asked.

The cop shook his head. "No."

"Did she handle the merchandise?"

"No."

"You have her fingerprints on the guns, the warehouse, the crates?"

"Not so far. Forensics is still working."

The desk sergeant leaned forward and pointed to the sign dangling above his head. "This is booking, not a courtroom. And I'm a sergeant, not a judge. Any chance we can we get her processed before a lineup forms?"

"Is she formally under arrest?" asked Dallas.

"Of course—"

"Think hard." Dallas stared at the arresting officer. "Did you *arrest* her? Or just bring her in for questioning? Do you have a warrant? Did you follow due process to the letter?"

The officer's gaze slid to the sergeant. "Sarge?"

Dallas stared at the sergeant with a you-don't-want-to-mess-with-a-high-priced-attorney-this-close-to-quitting-time expression on his face.

"Kick her loose," said the sergeant.

"What about me?" the man beside her sputtered. "If her arrest was bogus, then mine—"

"You wanna share a cell with Buba Junuh?" asked the sergeant, waving his pencil in the direction of the man's nose. "You just keep talking."

The man swallowed, his Adam's apple bobbing once as he suddenly became fascinated by the scarred, wood countertop.

"Make sure your client doesn't leave town," the sergeant warned Dallas.

"No problem," Dallas quickly replied.

As soon as Shelby's cuffs were off, he hustled her toward the door. He was getting out while the getting was good. He wasn't about to give the officers time to reconsider and end up stuck in a dingy interview room for the next four hours.

He had things to do, places to go.

"Thanks." Shelby gasped, struggling to keep up with his long strides.

They burst through the door into a spring evening and some comparatively fresh air. Dallas breathed a sigh of relief.

Finally. His duty was done. Another couple of hours at the office and he could grab dinner at Sebastian's on the way home and let life get back to normal.

The damp pavement glowed under the streetlights as the commuter crowd spilled from the El Station onto the street. A couple of middle-aged men in business suits gave Shelby speculative looks.

Dallas tossed them a don't-even-think-about-it glare. "You got cab fare home?" he asked her.

She rubbed her arms against the growing chill. "Of course I've got...oh, no..." She stopped short. "My *purse!*"

Dallas stared down another passerby. This one looked like a construction worker, with a navy work shirt and a black lunchbox. Didn't this woman know not to wander the streets of Chicago in a miniskirt?

"I left my purse at the Game-O-Rama," said Shelby.

"So, have the taxi stop and get it."

"They locked it up. I don't have a key. Gerry has the key."

Dallas tipped his head back, stared at the streetlamp and swallowed a few cusswords. Why him?

His dad might have taken on every stray south of

Jackson Park with a decent sob story, but Dallas definitely wasn't his father. He'd never be that naive.

With no other choice, he shrugged out of his suit jacket and dropped it around Shelby's shoulders. "Don't talk to anyone until I get back."

She nodded, glancing around the damp, darkening street.

The male pedestrians lurked in the shadows like a pack of jackals, and Dallas could almost feel his father's genetic code springing to life inside him.

He tamped down the silly urge to keep her close. They'd made it out of there by the legal skin of their teeth. There was no way he was taking her back inside.

Shoot.

Damn.

He let out a chopped sigh. Forget the key to the Game-O-Rama. "I'll get us a cab."

2

DALLAS SLAMMED THE DOOR behind her and strode around to the driver's side, while Shelby swore she'd never complain about taxis again. It was *so* much nicer in here than in the police car—a cushioned seat, handles on the inside of the doors, a window that opened, and no lurking aroma of vomit, sweat or urine.

She glanced at her watch, wishing she'd thought about her purse on the way out of the Game-O-Rama. Who knew when she'd get it back? Not that she could have managed to grab her purse with the cuffs on. And not that the young cop was likely to have helped her.

The opposite door opened and Dallas slid inside—six feet two, gray eyes, short, dark hair and a set to his jawline that said he'd rather be cleaning his oven than escorting her home.

Had she thanked him? Should she thank him? It wasn't like his help had come cheap. And she was already planning to dip into her meager savings to pay half of Allison's rent at the end of the month.

She guessed she could kiss that new pair of Bjorn shoes in Holstead's window goodbye. Along with the matching leather purse. It was a great sale, too.

She sighed inwardly. "How much do I owe you?"

"Forget it," said Dallas, slamming his own door.

"What do you mean, forget it? That was ten minutes' work. I figure it's fifty bucks, easy."

He turned and stared at her from beneath slanted brows. She got the feeling his clients didn't usually try to press money on him.

"What's your address?" he asked.

Shelby glanced at her watch again. Five-fifteen. Allison would have left for Balley's by now, and Shelby's apartment key was in her purse with the rest of her worldly goods. Too bad Flower-Fresh closed at five. Or was that five-thirty?

She leaned forward to talk to the driver through the open, Plexiglas barrier between the seats. "Can you take me to Black and Wheeler?"

"Allison lives on Rupert," said Dallas.

"Flower-Fresh is on the corner," she explained to the cabbie. "I need to pick something up."

Dallas sat back in his seat. "You're picking up your dry cleaning?"

"I sure hope so."

The cab lurched forward.

"Let me get this straight," said Dallas. "You just got arrested, narrowly avoided a stay in the lockup, you have no purse, no money. I'm assuming you've lost your job, and the first thing you need to do is *pick up your dry cleaning?*"

Shelby didn't get the connection. She blinked at him. "Yeah." She knew her credit card number. Hopefully that would be enough to spring the dress.

His forehead furrowed, he stared at her as if she was a bug under a microscope.

"I'm meeting Allison at Balley's," Shelby elaborated, gesturing to her wrinkled skirt and dusty tank top. "It's not like I can show up like this."

Dallas was silent for a full minute. "Right."

"You mind waiting?" she asked. "I could walk to Balley's from Flower-Fresh, but it's nearly a mile."

"Of course I'll wait."

Shelby smiled. "Thanks. And thanks for getting me out of jail."

"You weren't in jail."

"Don't you mean 'you're welcome'?"

He didn't smile at her joke. "Of course."

"I *can* pay you for your time," she felt compelled to offer. She didn't want him to think she was a charity case. Even if she nearly was.

His lips pursed as though he'd just sucked a lime. "You're Greg's fiancée's roommate—"

She grinned irreverently. "Which means we're practically cousins?"

She wasn't sure, but she thought he might have growled at that.

"Flower-Fresh on your right," said the cabbie.

Shelby peered hopefully out the window, but she was disappointed with what she saw. The sign was turned off and the front window was dark. But wait, somebody was on the sidewalk locking the front door. If she hurried...

She ripped off her seat belt and flung open her door before the cab had a chance to roll to a stop.

"Christ," Dallas bit out, reaching for her.

But she was quick enough to elude his hand.

She dashed between two parked cars and up onto the curb. "I need my dress," she called to the short, gray-haired woman with a set of keys in her hand.

"We're closed," said the woman, adjusting a plastic rain hat as she turned to walk away.

"You don't understand," said Shelby, following. "I need my dress."

The woman quickened her clicking steps on the wet concrete. "Come back tomorrow."

"But—"

"We're *closed*."

Shelby grasped the woman's arm in an effort to force her to listen.

The woman spun. She tilted her chin, eyes turning to black beads, voice going snappish. "Do I have to call the cops?"

Dallas's deep voice sounded behind Shelby. "I'd consider it a personal favor."

The woman looked up. Her eyes widened and her lined face instantly softened.

Dallas reached past Shelby and handed the woman a folded bill. "If you wouldn't mind?"

A tense half smile formed on the woman's face. She whisked the money from Dallas's hand. "Why not?"

"You trying to get arrested again?" Dallas muttered to Shelby as they followed the woman to the door.

Shelby didn't answer, figuring it was a rhetorical question.

The woman's large key ring jangled as she worked her way through the three dead bolts. She turned to Shelby and held out her hand. "Ticket, please."

"I uh, lost my purse," said Shelby.

The woman glared at her in exasperation. "You're not gettin' nothing without a ticket."

"It's an emerald dress." Shelby gestured to her neck and shoulders. "Scooped neckline, cap sleeves. I'll recognize it when I see it."

"No ticket. No dress." The woman turned the key back in the top lock.

Dallas sighed hard next to Shelby. He handed the woman another bill. "Emerald," he said. "Scooped neckline. And she'll recognize it when she sees it."

"I'll pay you back," Shelby whispered to Dallas as the woman slipped through the door and shut it firmly in their faces.

"Forget it," said Dallas. "Greg can—"

"No. I'll take care of—"

"I was going to say Greg can be my errand boy for the next week or so."

Shelby glanced up at Dallas's poker face. A sense of humor? It was hard to tell. Just in case, she responded in a lighthearted tone. "Or I could be your errand boy."

The expression in his eyes suddenly shifted. It went from cold to hot in half a heartbeat, and her nervous system reacted with a flutter. Holy cow. Apparently serious, cynical, arrogant lawyers were good for more than one thing.

The door behind her clattered open, and the dry cleaner shoved a film-covered dress into her hands.

"That's it!" Shelby cried. *Yes.* Finally, something was going right today.

The woman harrumphed and turned to relock the door.

Dallas lifted the dress from Shelby's hands. "Come on. Let's go before the taxi takes off."

DALLAS WATCHED Shelby's back as she dashed across the packed, brightly lit parking lot of Balley's. There was a lineup at the door and no guarantee that Allison was even inside. If she wasn't, space cadet Shelby was stuck in a nightclub parking lot with nothing but a change of clothes to her name.

Not that the woman was Dallas's responsibility. He'd already gone *way* above and beyond the call of duty. Not even Greg could complain he hadn't.

Dallas had a pile of work waiting at the office and a dinner reservation at Sebastian's for eight o'clock. Sebastian's was wildly popular, and he'd had the reservation for two weeks. He needed to scope out the place before he took his soon-to-be most important clients there next week.

He had things to do, places to go. If Shelby Jacobs wanted to line up outside Balley's on the off chance that Allison was inside, that was her choice. She was a grown woman, perfectly capable of asking for help, even using the telephone if it all went sideways.

He found himself focusing on her long, sexy legs. Hell, any one of the hundred or so guys inside would probably give his eye teeth for the chance to drive her home.

Dallas paused.

Dammit. There went the Williams do-gooder gene again.

He reached into his pocket to grab some money, then stuffed it into the taxi driver's hand.

"Thanks," he muttered as he hauled himself out of the car, shrugging back into the suit jacket Shelby had abandoned on the seat between them.

He adjusted his collar and straightened his tie. Rain began to sprinkle down as he lengthened his strides toward the nightclub lineup. He eased in beside Shelby, feeling the base beat that throbbed right through the wall of the building.

She looked up at him quizzically. "What are you doing here?"

Dallas lifted the dress out of her hand as he met the gaze of the man in front of her. The man hesitated, then looked away. *Too bad, buddy. Just not your night.*

Dallas leaned over and spoke in a low tone. "I wanted to make sure you found Allison."

Shelby pulled back and grinned, her changeable eyes sparkling lime-green in the streetlights. "What? You think I need a baby-sitter?"

Dallas could feel the interested stare of the man in front of them. The rain was increasing and the lineup wasn't moving. What the hell was he doing here anyway?

Shelby was hardly a babe in the woods. For all he knew, she really was a petty criminal. He couldn't exactly picture her selling a bazooka. But pirated software? Maybe a con artist? Hell, she had *him* eating out of the palm of her hand.

Out of the corner of his eye he saw a bouncer moving the length of the lineup. Once again, he reached into his jacket pocket and pulled out a bill. A big one this time.

He slipped it into the man's palm. "Can you get us inside?"

The burly man, glanced down into his palm. "Follow me."

Dallas grabbed Shelby's hand, towing her along before she could ask any questions, keeping his eyes front as they cut the lineup at the door.

"Is there anyone you can't bribe?" asked Shelby.

"Not so far," said Dallas. Though it wasn't part of his daily routine. This had to be the most expensive *nondate* he'd ever been on.

Warm air, an eclectic mix of perfumes and a blast of sound from the band met them in the crowded foyer.

"See Allison?" Shelby asked, coming up on her toes and tipping her chin.

Dallas tucked her in behind him, shouldering a path toward the dance floor. "Stay close," he called back.

"Absolutely," she shouted, tucking her fingertips into the waistband of his slacks.

His muscles contracted at the unconsciously sexual gesture. She was simply trying to keep from getting crushed by the crowd, he told himself. If she was trying to flirt, he had a feeling he'd know it.

To his immense relief, he quickly spotted Allison at a table near the dance floor. He headed straight toward it.

"Dallas?" Allison's eyes went round.

Then she peeked around him. "Shelby?"

Shelby groaned and plunked herself down on a chair. She picked up Allison's martini and took a healthy swallow. "I've just had the worst day of my life."

Allison drew back, gazing at Shelby with interest as she tucked her long dark hair behind one ear. "Given your life, that's saying something."

Shelby nodded vigorously. "Oh, yeah. Even for my life, it was bad. But first things first. I need to freshen up. Can I borrow your purse?"

"Sure." Allison handed her a small black bag that matched her sparkling dress.

Shelby got to her feet, taking the emerald dress from Dallas's hands. "I'll tell you all about it after I change." Then she melted into the crowd.

Allison turned her attention to Dallas. "Do you know where Greg is?"

"Last time I saw him, he was at the office."

Allison held out her hand. "Can I borrow your cell phone?"

"Of course." Dallas fished it from his jacket pocket.

"He's late," she said, pressing the buttons on his phone.

A cocktail waitress appeared at Dallas's side. "Get you a drink?"

"No—"

"Another martini," said Allison, holding the phone to her ear. "Make it two. You want one, Dallas?"

Dallas started to shake his head.

"Make it three," said Allison.

Dallas gave up and sat down. It had cost him fifty bucks to get in the door. He might as well have a drink before he left.

"Greg?" said Allison, raising her voice and covering her opposite ear. "Where *are* you?"

There was a pause.

"I've been at Balley's for half an hour. Dallas and Shelby are here."

She glanced at Dallas, shrugging her shoulders. "Beats me."

Then she paused again, her expression growing irritated as the seconds ticked by.

"But we talked about..."

She shook her head. "No."

Another pause. "No. Not if you want to live."

Her frown deepened. *"Greg."* She drew his name out on a groan of exasperation.

Dallas feigned an interest in the couples gyrating on the dance floor, swearing off fiancées then and there. If a guy had to put up with whining in exchange for getting his work done on a Friday night, Dallas wanted no part of it.

"Fine," said Allison tersely.

Dallas zeroed in on the band. They were pretty good.

"Right," she added.

He squinted trying to make out the name stylized on the bass drum.

"Later," she finished.

Elipso...something.

She clicked the phone shut and handed it back to Dallas, catching his gaze with her wounded blue eyes.

Oh, crap. He didn't want to ask.

He *really* didn't want to ask.

Luckily, Shelby appeared through the crowd.

Thank goodness. No, wait. He sucked in a tight breath. Not thank goodness. This was bad, too.

The shimmering emerald dress molded to her curves like a lover, showing off rounded breasts, a flat stomach, cascading over her smooth hips to mid-thigh. There was no way in the world she was wearing underwear beneath it. The realization jacked up his heart rate.

She'd pulled her hair up into a tousled bun and put on just enough makeup to deepen the color of her eyes—jade-green as they reflected the dress. Her cheekbones stood out. Her lashes were thick and lush and dark, and her full lips were something out of a midnight fantasy.

At least a dozen heads swiveled to follow her progress across the polished floor. Dallas swallowed.

The waitress set the drinks down on the table—not a moment too soon. He handed the woman his credit card and took a swig of his martini.

Shelby wriggled her way into the seat between him

and Allison. "That's better," she sighed, scooting a little closer to the small, glass table. She picked up her own martini and crossed one gorgeous leg over the other, seeming genuinely oblivious to the stares of the men all around her.

"So, tell me what happened," said Allison, recovering quickly from her conversation with Greg.

Shelby sucked her olive off the toothpick.

Dallas shifted in his chair.

"I lost my purse and didn't have taxi fare," she said.

Talk about burying the lead. Dallas crunched down on his own olive.

"Well, it's not exactly lost," she continued. "But it's locked up in the Game-O-Rama. I don't know when I'm going to get it back."

"Go tomorrow," said Allison.

Shelby shook her head. "I also lost my job."

Allison sat back. "Oh, no. What did you do?"

"Nothing. My boss got arrested."

Dallas wondered when the heck she was going to get to the part where *she* got arrested. Then he wondered why Allison automatically assumed Shelby had done something to get fired. Then he started wondering about Shelby's honesty all over again.

Had she lost jobs before? Maybe pilfered merchandise from her employer?

"So how'd you end up with Dallas?" asked Allison, nodding his way.

Shelby grinned. "He bailed me out of jail."

"I didn't bail you out of jail," Dallas corrected. "You weren't *in* jail."

Shelby leaned forward, giving an almost illegal view of her cleavage. "They arrested me, too. Slapped the cuffs on and everything." Then she leaned sideways and nudged his shoulder, giving him a secretive smile.

He tried to keep his gaze under control, really he did. But a quick glance downward confirmed his suspicions that she was sans brassiere and in terrific shape.

"Dallas was great," she said, her words turning rapid-fire as she straightened away from him. "He made them let me go. Then he bribed, like, everyone in the world to get me here so I could drink with you."

Allison slanted Dallas a suspicious look.

What? A guy couldn't be a good Samaritan these days?

"I simply pointed out to the officers at the Haines Street lockup that their case against her was shaky," he said.

"You *bribed* the cops?" asked Allison.

"I did not bribe the cops." He took a swallow of his martini. "I bribed the dry cleaner."

"And the bouncer," said Shelby.

"I *tipped* the bouncer," said Dallas.

"And here we are," said Shelby, leaning back with a happy sigh, draping her arms across the back of her chair as though all was suddenly right with her world. "Where's Greg?" she asked Allison.

Something flashed briefly in Allison's eyes. "Working late."

Which was where Dallas should be, instead of taking mental liberties with Shelby's body. Which was where he was going to go, right now before he disgusted himself further. He downed the rest of his martini.

A man tapped Shelby on the shoulder, and Dallas fought an urge to smack the guy's hand away.

"Like to dance?" the man asked her.

"Sure," said Shelby, rising to her feet.

"Care for another?" asked the waitress.

"Sure," said Dallas as his gaze rested on the smooth skin reveled by the plunging V at the back of her dress—his and fifty other gazes with even less noble intentions. He probably owed it to Greg and Allison to make sure Shelby survived the evening.

He'd work all day Saturday to make it up.

COFFEE MUG STEAMING on Allison's Formica kitchen table on Saturday morning, Shelby drew a red felt pen circle around an ad for a balloon delivery agent. Heck, she was a responsible adult, cheerful, enthusiastic, a self-starter, and she was willing to wear costumes.

Allison appeared in the doorway, leaning sideways against the white-painted jamb while she covered a wide yawn with the palm of her hand. Her dark hair was disheveled, and her flannel nightgown drooped off one shoulder. Faint traces of her mascara were smudged beneath her squinting eyes.

"What the hell are you doing up so early?" she asked. Then she spotted the coffeepot and made a beeline.

"Looking for a new job," Shelby answered. "You suppose a balloon delivery agent would have to wear fishnet stockings?"

Allison poured a steaming mug of Costa Rican blend. "Ahh," she sighed, inhaling deeply, closing her eyes and cradling the mug as if it were a magic elixir. "I'd say yes."

"To the fishnet stockings or the coffee?"

"Both." She headed for the table. "Fishnets, French maid uniform, sexy nurse outfit, you name it. And you'd probably have to learn to sing Happy Birthday like Marilyn Monroe."

"I could do a clown outfit. Deliver balloons to kids." Shelby wasn't so crazy about the erotic slant. She looked Allison up and down. "You look like hell, you know?"

"I was two martinis ahead of you. And I was pissed at Greg." She slumped into one of the chairs. "It's not my fault."

"Of course it's not." Shelby circled another promising ad. This one for a café waitress. It was the breakfast shift. God, she hated the breakfast shift. "Your fiancé stood you up. The evening had to suck."

"At least I didn't get thrown in jail."

"Now *that* is an excellent point." Shelby circled an ad for a dental assistant. Not that she had any desire to stick her hands in strangers's mouths. But they were willing to train the right person.

Allison took a careful sip of her coffee. "You know, I love having you around as a barometer."

"Who wouldn't?" asked Shelby, scanning for anything else that was promising. Not much to choose from. She sighed and dropped the felt pen. "Compared to me, even Joyce Vinton is a success story."

"I heard she's doing makeup parties in Boise now."

"See what I mean? What was it we voted her in high school?"

"'Most likely to be photographed with snakes.'"

Shelby shook her head, fighting a grin. "We were *so* crude."

"That we were, Miss Most Likely To Marry Money More Than Once."

"I'm still waiting for the first time." Shelby scanned

down the column of want ads one more time, just in case. "Think I'd make a good custodian?"

"Bad choice."

"They get to work nights."

"If you want to marry money, you need to hang around rich guys."

"Neil was rich. Look where that got me."

"Neil was a slimeball, and the Terra Suma lounge was a dive."

"He pulled in thousands of dollars a night."

"And blew it all on expensive liquor and horse racing." Allison had had enough e-mails and phone calls from Shelby over the past year to know about Neil's shortcomings.

"Well, that's true enough." Shelby had to agree.

"You need a job that puts you in contact with classy guys."

"Balloon deliveries?"

Allison sat up straight and her eyes lit up. "I know."

"What?"

"*I* can get you a job."

Shelby shook her head. "You will *not*. You've done enough already."

Shelby was determined to take control of her own life. And, she still had her pride. Of course, that was only because they hadn't strip searched her yesterday.

Allison didn't give up. "But, it's a great—"

"No," said Shelby with another firm shake of her head. "Whatever I do, whatever I decide, it's going to be me this time, just me."

Allison stood up and went for the phone. "Let me give Greg a quick call."

Shelby jumped up from her chair. She scooted across

the room and scooped the phone from Allison's hand. "You're not baby-sitting me anymore. Bad enough that you're giving me a roof over my head."

Allison grinned and cocked her head to one side. "Thought you said you were kicking in for rent."

Shelby backed away, clutching the phone to her chest. "Of *course* I am." She glanced down at the newspaper. "Just as soon as I get the balloon delivery job."

Allison took a few steps forward. "That'll be nothing but slimy men ogling your legs and pulling you into their laps. How're you going to meet anybody decent?"

Shelby gave a little shudder. She'd fended off plenty of hands in her cocktail waitress job. She didn't particularly look forward to it again. "Okay, I'll take the job at the diner."

Allison turned the paper so it was facing her and read the circled ads. Then she looked back up at Shelby, raising her eyebrows. "You? Get up at 5:00 a.m.? I don't think so," she scoffed.

"Then I'll be a custodian. They work nights."

Allison made a face. "Scrubbing urinals?"

Shelby felt her own expression crumple into one of distaste.

"After last night," said Allison. "Greg owes me *big* time."

"He owes *you*, not me."

"Yeah, but he's got nothing I want for me." She paused. "Well, except for the obvious."

Shelby smiled. "His heart. His soul. And everything he owns or ever will own?"

"Exactly. But those came with the ring. I need something more before I'm ready to forgive him. And I happen to know that they need a new receptionist at Turnball, Williams and Smith."

Shelby shrank back and shook her head. "Uh-uh." She was not about to let Allison exploit her fiancé to get her a job.

"Day shift," said Alison. "Office opens at eight-thirty."

Shelby steeled herself against the temptation. She was making it on her own. If nothing else, for the sake of her ego. She was twenty-five years old, and her life was bordering on pathetic.

"Air-conditioned in the summer, heated in the winter," sang Allison.

"I'm doing this *myself*."

"Classy clients. Rich, classy clients."

"I have my pride."

"Regular breaks, medical benefits and a pension plan."

Shelby gritted her teeth. This was cruel and unusual temptation. With a job like that, she wouldn't be pathetic. She might even be successful.

"Coffee bar on the main floor," said Allison.

Shelby felt herself weaken.

Obviously sensing victory, Allison held out her hand for the phone, wiggling her fingers. "Frappino's. Mochaccinos every day of the week."

That did it. Shelby groaned and handed over the phone. "Fine. Exploit away."

Not that she expected Greg to say yes. He'd be crazy to hire her. She didn't know the first thing about being a classy receptionist. But she'd sleep better at night if he turned her down, instead of *her* thumbing her nose at the job of a lifetime and then wondering forever what might have been.

Allison took the phone, waving it around for emphasis. "It's not exploitation. It's not even nepotism. Any job placement agency will tell you to use your contacts. And I'm your contact in Chicago. *Use* me."

"Make sure you tell him I don't know the first thing about being a receptionist."

Allison grinned as she punched in a number and lifted the phone to her ear. "I won't lie. Greg Smith, please."

Shelby's stomach tightened into a knot.

"Hey, how hard can it be?" asked Allison. "You answer a few phone calls, greet a few clients, file a few folders. You do know the alphabet, right?"

"I still sing it inside my head."

Allison grinned, raking her messy dark hair across her scalp and shaking her head. "Greg?" she said into the phone.

"What?" she asked almost immediately.

She paused. "Because Shelby woke me up."

Allison winked at Shelby. "Yes, she is very punctual."

Shelby's palms turned sweaty as, despite herself, she started to hope. A cushy job in a law office sounded so much better than delivering balloons in a French maid's outfit or slinging hash at 5:00 a.m.

Some women just weren't cut out for 5:00 a.m. Unless, of course, it had been a really great party.

"Of course I'm not mad," Allison said into the phone. "Shelby did a *fantastic* job of entertaining me last night." She gave a theatrical sigh. "Otherwise I would have been *so* lonely in the club all by myself."

Shelby rolled her eyes.

Allison grinned unrepentantly as she listened to Greg's response. "As a matter of fact, there *is* a way to thank her. She's looking for a job as a receptionist."

Now that was a stretch. Shelby was looking for a job requiring a warm body.

"Experience?" asked Allison. "Absolutely."

Shelby's eyes widened and she shook her head, making a slashing motion across her throat. Allison had promised not to lie.

"She's worked with the public for years," said Allison. "She's greeted customers, handled cash, balanced expenses. She's good with details, extremely organized and very personable."

Shelby had to admit, it was all *basically* true. If keeping twelve drink orders straight counted as being organized.

"Debbie's old job? Now why didn't I think of that?"

Shelby bit down on her bottom lip, afraid to let herself hope.

"She can start on Monday... Of course... Bye, sweetheart."

Allison hung up the phone and Shelby let out a sharp gasp, trying not to let terror overwhelm her excitement. She had a job. A *real* job.

"You're in," said Allison with a wide smile.

"I can't believe you pulled that off."

"Believe it."

"You're incredible."

"And you're going to be great. You've already met Dallas and Greg. And Allan, the other partner, is a pussycat."

3

DALLAS NODDED to his partner, Allan Turnball, as he strode across the newly decorated reception area of Turnball, Williams and Smith, briefcase in one hand and a double mochaccino in the other. He loved Monday mornings—loved it when an entire week of untapped possibilities stretched out in front of him.

He had a meeting with Eamon Perth at ten, lunch with Judge Weinberger, and he was hooking up with Greg for racquetball and a beer before he caught the Cubs game on ESPN.

If he could convince Eamon Perth to put them on permanent retainer, he could announce the coup to Greg tonight, giving Greg bragging rights for his meeting with Preston International in New York on Friday. A couple of cornerstone clients like Perth-Abercrombie and Preston International, and the sky would be the limit for their budding law firm.

As Mondays with possibilities went, it didn't get much better than this.

He headed toward the hallway that led to his office, but caught a bright flash in the corner of his eye, bringing him to a stop. Something was out of place.

He slowly turned toward the receptionist's desk, and his mouth dropped open a notch as he stared at a pair of black, spike-heeled pumps, impossibly long legs, a shiny gold dress over a perfectly rounded rear end, and a head of riotous, auburn hair barely tamed in a knot.

His mouth went dry as last night's dream popped, full blown, into his mind. His palm turned slick against his briefcase handle.

Allan appeared at his side. "Did you meet our new receptionist?"

Something settled like a lead weight in Dallas's stomach.

The woman pivoted to face him and he nearly dropped his coffee onto the three-week-old, hand-knotted, golden-onyx carpet.

"Dallas Williams," said Allan. "This is Shelby Jacobs."

Shelby's bright red lips curved into a friendly smile. The silky-smooth lines of the gold dress hugged her knockout figure. Gathered, capped sleeves barely covered her shoulders, and a heavy zipper was pulled just low enough to stimulate his imagination.

"What the...?" He barely sputtered out the question before his vocal chords shut down in sheer incredulity.

"We've met," said Shelby. "Great to see you again, Dallas."

Dallas? What were clients going to think when the receptionist called the partners by their first names? What were clients going to think when the receptionist looked like she belonged on a Vegas runway?

He glanced at the newly decorated wall behind her—its arched, Italian bookcase, leather-bound law books, bronze-and-marble statues, the wing chairs, the fresh flowers and the custom oil paintings that nearly screamed class and success. Then he looked back at

Shelby—sexy, spectacular, totally inappropriate, Shelby.

Was this a *joke*? He turned his horror-stricken face to Allan. Blinking, waiting for the man to burst out laughing.

He didn't.

"Can I get you anything?" asked Shelby, shifting in Dallas's peripheral vision. "Coffee? Files?" She gestured to the bookcase behind her. "A reference book?"

Dallas spoke to Allan through clenched teeth. "Can I see you in my office for a moment? Bring Greg."

He turned to take one more look at Shelby. He'd found the woman in *handcuffs*. In the Haines Street lockup. He wasn't even sure she was innocent. And even if she didn't steal the artwork from their walls, they sure as hell couldn't make *her* the first thing clients saw when the entered Turnball, Williams and Smith. Clients like Eamon Perth.

Eamon Perth.

Good God, Dallas had less than two hours to get her out of here.

With the barest of nods in her direction, he strode into his office, resisting the urge to slam his leather briefcase down on the polished desktop.

Greg entered behind him, closely followed by Allan.

"What's going on?" asked Greg affably.

Dallas turned to glare at him. "You hired a receptionist without even *talking* to me?"

Allan quickly closed the office door.

"Allison said you'd met her, and you seemed to like her," said Greg.

Dallas moved behind his cherrywood desk, bracing

his hands on the high back of his chair. "I met her in the *Haines Street lockup.*"

"But they didn't arrest her."

"Only because *I* was there."

"Allison asked me to thank you for that."

Dallas bit back an unflattering observation about Allison's influence over Greg.

Allan took a step forward. "She seems very nice."

"*Nice?*" Dallas's voice came out strangled. "Did you check her references? Her police record?" Had they even bothered to step back and take a good, long look at the woman?

Greg straightened. "Her police record?"

"When I met her Friday night, she was under arrest."

"She doesn't have a police record. She's Allison's roommate. From college."

Allan stepped in again. "I think we should give her a chance."

Dallas couldn't believe they were ganging up on him. He rounded the desk and brushed past them both, opening the office door and gesturing out into the reception area.

He kept his voice low. "Has it occurred to the two of you that *she* is the first person our clients are going to *see* when they walk in?"

Greg and Allan both peered out.

"So?" asked Greg.

"I don't get it," said Allan.

"Am I the only one who cares about making a professional impression?" asked Dallas.

"She is kind of pretty," said Allan. "But I don't see how—"

"*Kind* of pretty?" asked Dallas.

"She's making Harold Bouthier smile," said Greg.

Dallas glanced out the door. For a second his heart stopped beating. "She's *flirting* with Harold Bouthier."

"That's not flirting," said Greg. "She's just being friendly."

Shelby laughed at something Harold had said, her green eyes lighting up. He leaned a little closer. She didn't back away, simply listened with interest.

"She's flirting," said Dallas.

"You can't even hear her," said Greg.

"With those legs, everything is flirting."

Both of his partners turned to stare at him in amazed silence.

"What?" asked Dallas. "You mean to tell me neither of you noticed her legs?"

Greg's face slowly broke into a grin. "I don't think we can legally discriminate against her based on the fact that you're a leg man."

Allan joined in, smacking Dallas on the shoulder. "Just keep a lid on it in the office there, Dallas."

"I'm not discriminating against her based on—"

"She's attractive, I'll give you that," said Greg. "Can't hold a candle to Allison, of course."

Dallas shot Greg a quizzical look. Allison was cute enough, but Shelby was in a whole other league. Clients were going to walk into walls while staring at her. Who knew how many personal injury claims they'd have to settle?

He quickly shook himself. "We're allowed to discriminate against her based on qualifications and experience."

"Allison says she's experienced," said Greg. "Maybe you should spend a little time on your personal life. Get out there on a few dates. You know, halve the testosterone concentration so that you don't—"

"This has nothing to do with my testosterone concentration."

Both of the other men looked unconvinced.

Dallas raked a hand through his hair. "Look. All I'm saying is that you had no right to hire an employee behind my back. I don't think she's suitable, and I think we need to—"

"Give the woman a chance," said Allan. "Bouthier likes her. Maybe it's because she's kind of pretty. But who cares?"

"*I* care."

"Well, you're just going to have to deal with your own libido," said Greg. "I promised Allison we'd give her a chance, and I've got Allan's backing."

Before he could protest again, both men left his office, Greg heading out to meet Bouthier, and Allan crossing the hall to the library.

Dallas glanced at his watch.

Fine. He still had over an hour before Eamon Perth was due. It couldn't be that hard to dissuade a woman like Shelby Jacobs.

"I DON'T THINK Dallas likes me much," said Shelby as she took a seat across from Allison in Frappino's on the first floor of the office building. It was her fourth day on the job, and things seemed to be going pretty well—other than the fact that Dallas had barely said two words to her. Well, except for Monday morning when he suggested she could get a better job.

He'd even offered to help her find one.

Not a good sign.

"Dallas can be tense," said Allison, stirring the foam into her coffee. Allison worked as a graphic artist across town, but today a meeting with a client had brought her close enough to meet up.

"It's more than that." Shelby tore off a piece of the cinnamon bun they'd agreed to share.

"Yeah?" Allison looked her in the eyes.

Shelby faltered, squinting at the red tinge and slight puffiness around Allison's eyes. "What's wrong?"

"Nothing." Allison waved a dismissive hand. "Tell me about Dallas."

"Forget Dallas. You look upset."

Allison shrugged, still toying with her stir stick. "Greg stood me up again last night."

Shelby dropped the chunk of cinnamon bun, wiping her sticking fingers on a paper napkin. "But you were out until after eleven. I heard you come in."

"I walked home. I was thinking... I don't know what I was thinking."

Shelby's heart contracted. "Allison..."

"It's his work. Always his work. We haven't had sex in two weeks." She glanced from side to side to make sure their conversation couldn't be overheard. Then she leaned across the table, pitching her voice below the general buzz of conversation. "How can I marry a man who doesn't want me?"

The question shocked Shelby. She had no idea that Greg's working was causing any more than a minor tiff. "He wants you. *Of course* he wants you."

"Then why is he always working?"

Shelby thought for a moment. "I know they're after a couple of big clients right now. There's Eamon Perth from Perth-Abercrombie—I haven't met him because all of Dallas's meetings have been outside the office. But it feels like he's really important.

"And there's the New York firm, Preston International. They've been doing a ton of research on them. And I know they just redecorated to impress clients. Maybe this is a temporary thing."

"I'm beginning to think *I'm* the temporary thing."

Shelby's heart went out to Allison. "I'm sure he misses you just as much as you miss him. Give him a little time."

"You're a lot more forgiving than me. I'm about ready to hand him an ultimatum."

Shelby felt her eyes go wide. "You can't mean break up with him? He's a wonderful guy."

"Either he shows up on our next date, and we have *great* sex, or he can take his ring and—"

Shelby started to panic. Allison and Greg loved each other. They were great for each other. She didn't want Allison to say anything that was hard to take back.

"I don't think you want to go with an ultimatum," she said.

"Well I can't think of anything else that will make an impression on his thick skull."

Shelby picked up her coffee, putting a teasing tone in her voice. "You know, you can catch more flies with honey than vinegar."

"What? Your grandmother say that?"

Shelby nodded. "All the time. Though I don't think she had premarital sex in mind."

"Ha. They had premarital sex back then. They just lied about it."

Shelby grinned. "They also played hard to get."

"You think I'm too available?"

Shelby nodded. "I think you need to make him wait on you. Oh. Even better. Whet his appetite and *then* make him wait."

"How the hell am I going to whet his appetite if I never see him? He's got meetings tonight, then he leaves for New York tomorrow morning."

"The Preston International thing?"

"Exactly. He'll be gone all the way through the weekend."

"So send something with him."

"What? Slip my panties into his suitcase?"

That was what Shelby had been about to suggest.

"He's got six pairs," said Allison. "Doesn't seem to be working."

"Sexy pairs?"

"No. White cotton. Of *course* they're sexy."

"Hmm."

"Yeah. Hmm." Allison tore off a chunk of the cinnamon bun.

"Could you go to New York?"

"How does *that* make him wait?"

"Good point."

Allison groaned around a bite of cinnamon bun. "And can you imagine how horrible it would be if he was at meetings all evening long while I waited in his hotel room?"

"Pathetic," Shelby agreed.

"Seriously. I'd be worse off than when I started."

Gaze resting on the mochaccino machine as it churned out another foam-topped coffee, Shelby searched her brain. "Phone sex?"

"He has call waiting on his cell."

Shelby coughed out an outraged laugh. "He wouldn't."

"He has."

"Tell me again why you're marrying this man?"

Allison laughed darkly, tipping forward as she shook her head. "He's charming, intelligent, gorgeous and hardworking." She straightened, flipped her hair back and groaned again. "He really is. I just have to figure out how to get back on top of his priority list."

"Pictures," said Shelby.

"Pictures?"

"Sexy pictures."

"What? Like a magazine?"

Shelby pointed at Allison with her index finger, warming to the idea. "Yeah. Just like a magazine. Only you."

Allison's jaw dropped. *"What?"*

"You. In sexy pictures. Hide them in his luggage. He stares at them for four days in New York, comes home, and voilà. Instant sex."

"I don't have any sexy pictures."

"Have some taken."

"By *who?*"

"Me, Dallas—"

"Dallas!"

"I'm joking. There are studios that do stuff like that. They even supply the clothes, the makeup, the props, the works."

"Props?" Allison squeaked. "I don't think I can do props."

"I meant a feather boa, a fur rug. Sexy, not smutty."

Allison looked skeptical.

"It'd work," said Shelby.

"I don't think I could—"

"We'll call around, find some place with a female photographer. They give you the negatives. Nobody but you and Greg will ever know about it."

Allison grimaced. "I really don't know if I could do it."

"Focus on the results."

"Could *you* do it?"

"Absolutely. For the right cause—I mean, the right guy—yeah, sure, why not? It's no different than doing a striptease in your bedroom. It's not like Greg's going to show them to anyone." She paused. "Uh, you do trust him on that, right?"

"Of *course*. He'd never share them." Allison shook her head. "Not in a million years."

Shelby sat back. "There you go. Want to use the pay phone in the lobby?"

"Turnball, Williams and Smith," said Shelby into the telephone at her desk.

"I need a lawyer," said the voice on the other end.

"Are you an existing client of Turnball, Williams and Smith?"

Greg walked out of the boardroom, and Shelby couldn't help but smile at the thought of the pictures Allison was tucking into his luggage this morning. She hadn't seen them, but Allison had described them last night, blushing deeply when she talked about the merry widow outfit and lying naked on a pool table.

Despite her bravado, Shelby wasn't so sure she could have done it herself.

"Allan Turnball handled my incorporation, but now I'm getting a divorce," said the man on the telephone.

Greg stepped into the reception area and shook the hand of his next client.

"I'm sorry, but Turnball, Williams and Smith doesn't handle family law," said Shelby.

"But—"

She typed a few words into her online directory. "We have an affiliate, Asher and Henderson. They'll be able to help you out."

"Can they get my financial records from Allan? I don't want that bitch to get her hands on—"

"Absolutely," inserted Shelby, wondering if family law might be more exciting than corporate law. "Their telephone number is 555-8736. Tell them you're Allan's client."

She hung up the phone as Greg and the man from the reception area disappeared into Greg's office, leaving the silver-and-cream wing chairs vacant in the reception area.

Shelby started to get up to straighten the magazine pile on the low, mirrored table, but her telephone rang again.

"Turnball, Williams and Smith."

It was Allison. Her voice was a muted whisper. "Houston, we have a problem."

Shelby spun around and sat back down. "What? The pictures weren't ready?"

"No. I've got them. I'm at Greg's."

"Thank goodness."

"But Greg took his luggage to work. I've got nowhere to plant them."

"He didn't bring it up here."

"I figure it's in his car."

"Why are you whispering?"

"I don't know."

"Do you have his car keys?"

"No."

"Shoot."

"I think we have to abort the plan."

Shelby glanced around the office. They couldn't give up now. Not when they were this close to giving Greg a case of raging sexual frustration for the next four days.

She spotted Greg's open briefcase through the boardroom doorway. "No, we don't. I can get to his briefcase."

"His briefcase?"

"Yeah. I'll plant the pictures in his briefcase. Meet me in the lobby."

"What if he opens it in a meeting?"

"So what? He's hardly likely to put them on the overhead."

"I don't know—"

"You bring the pictures. I'll do the rest." It was a good plan. It was a great plan. They couldn't let the first little logistical complication shut them down.

There was a moment of silence on Allison's end of the phone. "You sure this is a good—"

"It's a *great* idea. Honey, you are going to drive him nuts."

"But what if he—"

"He won't. It'll be fine."

"If you're sure."

"Trust me. From what you described last night, it's a slam dunk. Meet me in the lobby in ten minutes."

"Right. I'm on my way."

Shelby asked one of the partner's secretaries to watch

the reception area for her, then she grabbed an elevator to the lobby.

Wearing sunglasses, a brimmed hat and a long coat, Allison slipped her a plain brown envelope. Shelby nearly laughed out loud at the espionage feel to the whole transaction.

Within minutes, she was back in the office.

It was a simple matter to meander into the boardroom, tuck the envelope under some file folders in the briefcase and slip back into her desk.

She was pretty good at this secret-agent stuff.

Her self-congratulations lasted all of two minutes.

Then Dallas headed into the boardroom, closed the briefcase, turned the locks, picked it up and headed for the front door.

Shelby shot out of her chair. "Where are you going?"

Dallas stopped short, staring at her with an incredulous expression.

"Where are you going *with Greg's briefcase?*" she elaborated.

Dallas's eye narrowed and he looked down. "This is my briefcase."

"No, it's not."

There was a moment of silence as his expression turned painstakingly patient. "Yes. Actually. It is."

Shelby's stomach went into a free fall. "But..."

She scrambled for a solution. Should she fess up and throw herself on his mercy? Surely he'd give the pictures back.

But then Allison would be mortified. Allison would probably kill her. She'd sworn on pain of death to keep Allison's secret.

Dallas gestured to the door. "If you don't mind, I've got an appointment."

For a brief second, she considered wrestling him to the ground. Too bad he was sure to win. Too bad she was sure to lose her job. She frantically searched her brain for an alternative.

"I'll be back in half an hour," he said, moving again, putting his hand on the doorknob.

"But, I thought..." She swallowed. She couldn't explain her mistake and ask for the pictures back without betraying Allison.

"Yes?" he asked.

"I put..." She whimpered under her breath.

"Is something wrong?"

"No," she squeaked. "Nothing."

"Good."

The door opened, then closed, and Dallas disappeared.

Shelby drew in a shuddering breath, forcing herself to mentally regroup. The pictures were pretty well buried in there. She had half an hour. She could still make it.

Plan C.

All she had to do was wait for Dallas to get back, get him out of his office, break into his briefcase and switch the pictures to Greg's. If Plan C worked out, Allison would never even suspect there'd been a problem.

4

WHEN DALLAS RETURNED to the office, he kept his eyes front to avoid looking at Shelby. If he didn't see her, he couldn't get those buzzing, inappropriate stirrings caused by her bedroom-tousled hair and the skimpy outfits she insisted on wearing. You would think the woman could look around and take her cue from the rest of the administrative staff.

But no. Today she was wearing a pair of low-cut blue pants with a button-up fly, a little nothing of a burgundy tank top printed with yellow and mauve flowers and inset with dark lace along the scooped neckline. The only thing he could say for it was she was definitely wearing a bra. But her heels were high, her legs were long, and the look in her eyes was always just a hair shy of a proposition.

He couldn't understand why the other partners didn't notice.

"Dallas," she called, setting down the phone and rising from her chair.

He ignored her, beelining for the relative safety of his office.

"Dallas?" she tried again, and he could hear her quick footfalls on the hallway carpet.

He dumped his briefcase on a chair near the door, and quickly positioned himself behind his desk, focusing his attention on a stack of papers.

"Dallas." She blew out a breath, and he gave in to the temptation to look up.

She stopped in the doorway, propping one smooth, bare arm against the doorjamb, smiling brightly. "I was wondering if you needed anything."

"Nope."

"Coffee? Water?" She came right into the office.

Dallas gritted his teeth against the hormonal rush. She was *not* the kind of woman he was attracted to. He went for class, sophistication and intelligence. She was raw sensuality and wild passion.

"Nothing," he said.

She moved even closer.

"Well, can I help you out here?" She straightened a couple of books on the far side of his desk.

"Don't—"

"I know you're busy, and things are getting a little untidy."

Dallas glanced around at his bare desk and his neatly organized office. "No, they're—"

"I could sort through your bookcase, make sure everything is in order. Maybe you could go and—"

"Shelby."

"What?"

"I *don't need* any help." And he didn't want her here. He wanted her *out there* where he didn't have to look at her, smell her sexy perfume, listen to her husky voice. The farther away the better.

"Oh." She took a step back.

In fact, the reception area wasn't nearly far enough.

He cleared his throat. "Have you given any thought to what we talked about?"

She looked puzzled. "We talked?"

Okay, good point, he'd pretty much avoided her since she started. "Monday," he elaborated. "About you getting another job. I mean, you don't want to be wasting your talents, and I'm sure you'd enjoy something a bit more stimulat—interesting."

"I *was* thinking about family law," she said.

"Family law?" Dallas had been thinking about rock music or high fashion. He wasn't sure anyone in the legal community was ready for Shelby.

She gave him a teasing smile. "You know, the interesting stuff. Who's cheating on who, who's in the will and who's out. The skeletons in the closets."

"*Interesting?* I call that sordid."

She shrugged and he fixated a second too long on her smooth shoulders. "Hey, I'm human. I'm interested in what makes people tick."

"So you like the tawdry, seamy side?"

"Hey, you like the snooty, boring side?"

"I prefer to think of it as class," he said.

"I prefer to think of it as repressed."

"I'm not repressed." The minute the words were out, he regretted the defensive tone. He didn't have to defend his career choices to her or anyone else. He was on track to success—more than he could say for her.

She didn't answer, but her expression challenged his assertion. He couldn't believe he was having this conversation with his receptionist.

He came out from around the desk, trying to herd her toward the door. "Okay, fine. I'm repressed. Thanks for your offer, but I don't need any—"

"What about your briefcase?" She shot toward the chair next to the door and picked it up. "Why don't I get it out of your way?"

Perfect, she was just inches from the doorway. Only seconds from now she'd be back outside.

"The briefcase is not in my way."

"It looks messy sitting on the chair," she insisted.

"It's fine." He reached forward, but she jerked it back out of his reach.

What the hell was her problem?

He took a firm step toward her and grasped the briefcase, his hand closing over hers, sending shock waves throughout his body.

"Let go," he insisted, stunned by the intensity of his reaction. He pulled the case toward him, fighting panic as his classy thoughts were replaced by tawdry ones.

She didn't let go but came *with* the briefcase, smack into the center of his chest. She tipped her chin, looking up at him with those wide eyes—jade color now, streaked with sapphire in the light of the office. They were mysterious, compelling, deeply sensual.

They both froze, and every sense he had zeroed in on her. Her skin was smooth, her hair fragrant, her lips full and dark, absolutely made for kisses—long, hard, inappropriate kisses, followed by sweaty, messy lovemaking that broke boundaries and bent rules.

His body hardened and his nerve endings snapped to attention.

A voice sounded in the hallway and panic shot through him. Reflexes took over but instead of stepping away from her, his hand smacked the door, pushing it shut to shield them from the prying eyes of the office staff.

The snap echoed through the room, followed by stunned and total silence.

He waited for her to step away, to cuss him out or

slap him for what he was thinking. But she didn't move, just stared up at him with a mixture of surprise and curiosity. Her thick lashes fanned over her eyes, and her soft lips parted slightly.

His mind screamed at him to step away from the gorgeous receptionist, but his body wanted to press closer. He sucked in gulps of oxygen, trying to stop the hand that was moving up her bare arm, brushing her satin skin with the backs of his knuckles. The contact was electric, and he felt it to his toes.

When he got to her shoulder, he touched her hair, running a few wisps through his fingertips, just to see if it was as soft as it looked. It was.

Somehow, his fingers got tangled in it, buried near the base of her skull. And then he was pulling her forward, dipping his head to meet her, inhaling her sweet breath.

His lips touched hers and sensation exploded. The briefcase slipped from his hand, and he reached up to touch her other cheek, cradling her soft face between his palms. She tasted sinfully sweet, like black coffee with swirls of sweet cream.

He opened his mouth, testing the seam of her lips with his tongue. A murmur sounded in the back of her throat, and she opened to accept him.

His hands slipped down her rib cage, skimming the sides of her breasts, finding the small seam between her low-cut pants and her stretchy tank top. He grazed his fingers along her taut belly, hitting a small delicate ring at her navel.

The sensation launched his hormones and he deepened the kiss, hauling her tight against him.

An alarm jangled in the back of his brain, as the sounds on the other side of the door penetrated.

He was in his *office*.

He was kissing *Shelby*.

He was breaking about a thousand ethical rules and at least a dozen laws.

He forced himself to let go of her. Then he eased back to break the kiss, giving in to an urge to stroke the pad of his thumb over her moist lips.

Then he stepped away, breathing hard. He didn't have the slightest idea what to say to either regain his self-esteem or keep himself out of court.

"You know what I'm talking about?" asked Shelby in a neutral tone that ignored what had just happened between them. "The interesting law-firm stuff. Like who's bopping their secretary during work hours."

In a split second flash, Dallas saw his entire career ending in a sexual harassment scandal.

Then he realized she was mocking him.

Here he'd been sucker-punched by his careening passion and his own ethical weakness, and she was making a joke.

"You need to change your shirt," he said sharply.

"My *shirt?*"

"There's a dress code here. No exposed navels." Particularly not those with a winking gold ring that was sure to invade his dreams tonight. "And think a little more conservative, please."

Shelby glanced down at her exposed midriff, but Dallas didn't dare.

Her jaw tightened, and she took a sharp breath. "Right. Fine." She put her hand on the doorknob, turning to leave.

"Shelby?"
"What?"
"My briefcase."

SHELBY STOMPED her way through the main floor lobby of the office building, tossing her shopping bag into the trash can and buttoning up the yellow satin blouse she'd bought at the department store across the street. So much for the briefcase caper.

She had no pictures.

She had no briefcase.

Dallas didn't like her clothes.

And she was *not* turned on by her boss. Uh-uh, no way, not going there ever again.

She pressed the elevator button, and the doors slid open immediately. Greg stepped out.

"Greg?"

"Hey, Shelby."

She was out of time? How could she be out of time? "Where are you going?"

"New York."

"So soon?"

"My flight's in two hours."

"But... Don't you..."

Greg cocked his head. "What?"

Shelby couldn't for the life of her come up with a way to make him stay.

Short of rushing upstairs, snatching Dallas's briefcase then chasing Greg to the airport, she didn't know how she was going to get the pictures into his luggage.

The odds of her making it out of the building before Dallas ran her down were not good. And the odds of making it to O'Hare before Greg checked his luggage were even worse. For a split second she considered fessing up to Greg. Maybe he'd help her retrieve the photos. At least they'd be out of Dallas's hands.

But they'd lose the element of surprise. And she would have failed Allison. There had to be another way.

She offered Greg a weak smile. "Have a good time."

"Everything okay upstairs?" he asked, concern clouding his expression. "You look upset."

"It's fine. It's great. I love the job."

"Don't let Dallas get you down."

She shook her head. "I won't."

"I think, deep down, he likes you."

Deep down, Shelby figured Dallas wanted to sleep with her. And for some reason, the thought horrified him. Probably something to do with her pierced navel. Or maybe he simply didn't consort with the employees.

Actually, she had to admire him for that.

"It's fine." She broadened her smile for Greg's benefit. "See you on Tuesday."

He gave her a wave as he headed for the exit.

As soon as he was out of sight, Shelby closed her eyes and groaned out loud.

Plan C had crashed and burned. She needed a Plan D.

She headed into Frappino's for some liquid inspiration. Liquor would have been better, but she ordered a large black coffee and found an empty corner table. She peeled off the lid and took a straight shot, letting the buzz and bustle of the coffee shop fade into the background.

Should she tell Allison that Dallas had the pictures before or after she rescued them? After would be *so* much better, but she couldn't put it off much longer without Allison getting suspicious. And she could hardly avoid answering the phone for the rest of the day.

"You work on the eighth floor, don't you?"

Shelby glanced up to see a pleasant-looking man in his midthirties standing beside her table.

"I've seen you in here before," he continued. Then he looked around at the crowded coffee shop and gestured to the empty seat across from her. "Do you mind?"

Shelby shook her head. "It's all yours."

"Randy Calloway," said the man, holding out his hand to shake.

Shelby briefly took his hand. "Shelby Jacobs."

"I work at Ryan, Finch and Finch across the street."

"Really? I'm with Turnball, Williams and Smith."

Randy grinned. "On the eighth floor."

"That's right."

"You a lawyer?"

Shelby shook her head. "Receptionist."

There was a twinkle in his eye. "Glad to hear it. I don't date lawyers."

Shelby raised her eyebrows. "Date?"

He gave her a shrug and a mischievous grin. "Call me an optimist."

Shelby shook her head. She'd seen guys like this a hundred times before, but after being dumped by Neil and hearing Dallas's criticism of her clothes, it felt good to have somebody try to flirt.

"How long have you worked there?" he asked.

"Just started this week."

"Got a boyfriend?"

Shelby grinned knowingly. "No."

"Work for any particular lawyer?"

"All of them."

"Looking for one?" he asked.

"Looking for one what?"

Randy leaned forward and lowered his voice. "A boyfriend."

Shelby leaned forward, too. "No."

"Is there a reason for that?"

"I'm a strong, independent woman who needs no man to be successful."

"You're a lesbian?"

Shelby laughed. "No."

Randy leaned back and picked up his coffee. "So I'm not completely dead in the water..."

"You're only on life support."

He clutched his chest. "Please, gorgeous lady, give me some oxygen."

Shelby couldn't help laughing. She started to gather her purse. "I have to—"

"Will you meet me tomorrow?" asked Randy, straightening and sobering.

Shelby shook her head as she rose. "Tomorrow is Saturday."

"Monday, then."

"You seem like a nice guy, but I'm not interested in dating."

"For coffee. Just coffee."

"Here?"

"Yeah."

Shelby shrugged. "Why not?" The rest of her day wasn't going to be a picnic. And if she ran afoul of Dallas again, she might appreciate Randy's ego boost on Monday.

Shelby waited until the reception area was quiet and empty. Allan was out at a meeting and Dallas was holed up in his office. He hadn't shown his face since he'd kissed her. Which was fine with Shelby. She didn't embarrass particularly easily, but no woman wanted to know that a man regretted touching her.

Not that it had been a bad kiss. In fact, it was a darn good kiss, considering it had been an impulsive, hurried, clandestine, mistake kind of thing. She wondered just how great a kisser Dallas would be when he was willing and put out a full effort.

Then she clamped down on that thought. Kissing the boss was a bad idea, particularly a boss who didn't want her working here.

Find her a new job where she wouldn't be wasting her talents? Ha. Find her a new job where he didn't have to look at her wardrobe was more like it.

Well, so sorry, Mr. Williams, but I'm all out of the librarian look. Nobody else seemed to mind her clothes. The partners' secretaries had been friendly, and the paralegals had even invited her to join them for coffee on Tuesday. She was hardly an outcast, fashion or otherwise.

She straightened her shoulders, putting her fingers over the telephone keypad, hesitating, taking a deep breath. Then she dialed Allison's phone number.

She owed it to her friend to be honest.

While the tone sounded in her ear, her stomach cramped. This was all her idea. She'd practically forced Allison into taking the pictures, and now she'd screwed up royally.

"Hello?"

"Allison?"

"Shelby? How'd it go? Does he have the pictures? He must be on the plane by now. Oh, God, I hope he doesn't open them while he's in flight—"

"Allison?"

"Yes?"

Shelby cringed. "I put the pictures in the wrong briefcase."

There was a silent pause. "You mean, he doesn't have them?"

"He doesn't have them."

There was another pause on the line, then a sigh. "Well, probably just as well. I would have been a nervous wreck waiting to see how he reacted—"

"Allison?"

"What?"

"I put them...in Dallas's briefcase."

"You what?" Allison shrieked.

Shelby jerked the phone from her ear for a second. "I'm *so* sorry. I thought it was Greg's. Greg was in the boardroom, and then he left, and it was the perfect opportunity, but then Dallas grabbed the briefcase and—"

"Get it back."

Shelby nodded. "Yeah. I will. I will."

Allison's voice turned to a high soprano. "I mean it, Shelby. You get those pictures back. And don't you dare let Dallas see them. Don't you dare even tell him I took them. Oh, my, God. How would I ever face him again?"

"I don't think he'd be shocked—"

Allison shrieked. "You've met him. He's Mr. Conservative. You can bet his girlfriends don't slip dirty pictures into his briefcase."

Allison had a point. Shelby was willing to bet Dallas's

girlfriends didn't even wear lingerie that showed their navels. They probably had full-length satin nightgowns, turned off the lights before stripping, then lay really still to keep from messing up their hair.

"Don't worry. I'll get them back. And I won't tell Dallas a thing."

"Do it right now."

"I'll do it right now."

"Phone me when you've got them. Then burn the damn things."

Burn them? Shelby was thinking more along the lines of overnight express to New York. Though maybe she'd wait a bit before mentioning that to Allison.

"I'll call you as soon as they're in my hands," she promised.

5

SHELBY WAS UP to something.

Dallas didn't know what or why, but she was flitting around his office like a felon.

She passed his office door for the third time in an hour and glanced inside. He didn't particularly want to hash over their kiss, so he made a show of picking up his telephone. She kept going.

He started to put the receiver back down, but his gaze caught the clock on the wall. It was three-thirty, on the last day of the month. Which meant he really did have a call to make.

To his father.

Although Jonathan Williams only lived an hour away, he and Dallas rarely saw each other. It was true they were both busy, but it was the need to tiptoe around each other's careers that kept them from making more of an effort to get together.

Still, Dallas refused to be one of those sons who ignored his only parent, so he'd pledged to himself that he'd call his dad at least once a month.

He inevitably put it off until the last day.

He dialed the office number and the ringing phone toned in his ear.

"Jonathan Williams's office."

"Hi, Nina. It's Dallas."

"Hey, Dallas. How's it going?" Nina had been his father's receptionist for five years, ever since he'd cleared her of a petty theft bust. Dallas strongly suspected she was also his lover and he assumed they kept things discrete because of Nina's three young children.

"I'm good," said Dallas. "Is Dad around?" Dallas always held out the small hope that his father would be busy or out of the office when he called. Then he would have done his duty without actually engaging in an awkward conversation.

"He's on the phone—"

"I'll—"

"But I'm sure he wants to talk to you." The line went silent.

Close, but no cigar. Dallas tapped a pencil against his desk, letting the rubber eraser act as a spring on the polished wood.

Shelby wandered by again, pausing by his door. When she saw he was still on the phone, she gave him a finger-waggling wave and continued on her way. Odd woman. She'd probably fit in just fine at his father's law practice. Dallas was pretty sure everyone who worked there had been arrested at one time or another.

"Hey, Dallas," came his father's voice.

"Hi, Dad."

"How are you today?"

"Just fine. You?"

"Couldn't be better. Just got off the phone with Kenny Hooper."

"The forger?"

"Now, Dallas, you know he was acquitted."

"Right." Which, in his father's eyes, made Kenny citizen of the year.

There was pride in his father's voice. "After the trial,

he took a community college course, and he just got a job as a graphic artist."

Dallas wondered if his father had simply helped Kenny emotionally or if he'd pitched in financially, as well. It was damn sure Kenny had never paid any legal fees.

Dallas forced a hearty note into his voice. "That's great to hear, Dad."

"Yeah. Well... How about you? What's on your caseload this month?"

"Embezzlement case for Perth-Abercrombie."

"The brokerage firm?"

Who else? "Yes."

"Nice work. Big money there." His father said it as though money was evil, and Dallas had been handed the case on a silver platter.

"Yes, there is," Dallas agreed, feeling his body tense up. Here Jonathan's real son was getting high-profile, high-paying cases, yet Jonathan's pride was reserved for Kenny, the quasi-adopted forger turned artist.

"Well, I'm sure you'll do a fine job for them."

"I hope so," said Dallas, wondering why he let his father's attitude disappoint him over and over again.

Shelby appeared in the hall.

"Looks like the receptionist needs me," said Dallas.

Her eyes widened slightly.

"Nice of you to call, son."

"Sure, Dad. Talk to you soon." Dallas hung up the phone.

"I didn't—" Shelby began.

"No problem." She'd inadvertently done him a favor. "Can I help you with something?"

She hesitated, a look of uncertainty crossing her face.

Maybe she was acting weird because they'd kissed. He knew he sure felt weird after kissing her.

After another moment's pause, she took a step into the doorway. She stood there, tapping her polished fingertips against her thumbs in sequential order, then reversing. The nervous expression disappeared from her face, replaced by one that looked rather calculating.

Oh, boy. What now?

Maybe this wasn't about the kiss.

Come to think of it, she didn't strike him as a woman who'd be thrown off balance by a kiss. She struck him as a woman who knew her kisses inside and out, and used them shrewdly.

In fact, she might have kissed him on purpose—to distract him. From...for example...his briefcase. She was rather obsessed with that briefcase. She'd asked about it earlier, and she had tried to take it away from him both before and after the kiss.

His briefcase...

Not that he could figure out what she could possibly want with it. It wasn't like he kept money there. There weren't even any salacious details of family law matters.

His most important case at the moment was an embezzlement prosecution for Perth-Abercrombie. And they were an accounting firm. Hardly the stuff of clandestine affairs and skeletons in the closet.

She finally spoke, all friendly and cheerful. "Would you like anything? Coffee? Bottled water?"

What was with the sudden beverage service today? Dallas started to say no, but then he decided to play along to see where it went. "Sure. Water would be fine."

But if the seal was broken, he was having it tested for knockout drops.

"Yeah?" she smiled. "Great. I mean, I'll be right back."

"Thanks," he called.

Two minutes later she was back with the water. A big bottle, still sealed. If not knockout drops, she must be trying to fill his bladder.

Dallas paused.

Smart girl.

He smiled, cracked the lid and took a long drink. "Thank you."

"You're welcome."

For a second he thought she was going to stand there and wait for it to make its way through his kidneys. He raised his eyebrows.

"I'll, uh—" she pointed behind her with her thumb "—just be outside if you need anything else."

Dallas held up the bottle in a toast. "You bet."

She backed out of the room.

Dallas leaned to one side, watching her walk back to her desk. The phone rang and she picked it up. She didn't transfer it, but talked for a few minutes to whomever was on the line.

He couldn't hear what she was saying, but it was clear from the way she glanced around the room and mangled the phone cord that the call was making her uncomfortable.

As soon as she hung up, he pressed her line and hit star sixty-nine.

"Ryan, Finch and Finch," said a pleasant woman's voice. "Randy Calloway's office."

"Sorry, wrong number," said Dallas, quickly hanging up. He clenched his jaw and cursed under his breath, suspicions blooming full-out in his mind.

Ryan, Finch and Finch were the defense team for the Perth-Abercrombie embezzlement case. His little receptionist was clearly up to something. Best case scenario, she was fraternizing with the opposition.

He should have gone with his gut instinct and left her in the Haines Street lockup. Though everyone was innocent until proven guilty in his world, his new receptionist chatting with Randy Calloway was *way* too much of a coincidence to ignore.

Dallas sat back in his chair, mentally brainstorming scenarios. What was going on? Had the whole thing been a setup?

Had she renewed her acquaintance with Allison in order to infiltrate Turnball, Williams and Smith? Would Ryan, Finch and Finch try something that complex? The law firm didn't have the greatest reputation in the world, but to send in a spy on a three-hundred-thousand-dollar embezzlement case?

Sure, their client had lost his job and would probably have to pay damages, but it was hardly Enron. Nobody was going to jail.

He picked up his pencil again and tapped it on the desktop, peering out into the reception area at Shelby who was nervously glancing around. Perhaps it was time to give her what she wanted and figure out what she was up to. He stood up from his chair and headed for the rest room.

He came back to a missing briefcase.

Damn.

He'd held out a small hope that he'd been wrong.

He headed for the reception area, coming to the edge of her desk.

She glanced up, eyes wide and guilty as sin. The woman couldn't bluff her way out of a paper bag. What the hell made her decide to take up crime?

He shook his head, walking around the desk to find his briefcase stuffed in beside her trash can. The locks were scuffed and she had a pair of scissors and a bent paperclip in her hand.

"Probably don't want to take up safecracking," he said, stepping back and motioning for her to precede him into his office.

"I..." She closed her eyes and shook her head.

"You are *so* busted," he whispered.

He picked up the briefcase and followed close behind her, afraid she might make a run for it.

She turned her head to look at him while she walked. "It's not what you think."

"Not what I think? Now where have I heard that before? Oh, I remember, the Haines Street lockup."

"This has nothing to do with—"

"Give it a rest. I caught you red-handed." He closed the office door behind them. He was suddenly angry at her callous disregard for her own safety. Did she *want* to go to jail?

"I'm sorry," she said.

"Sorry?" he nearly yelled. "You think sorry cuts it? I could call the cops right now and have you thrown in jail."

She blanched. Probably had memories of the last time they hauled her away in cuffs. Good.

"For trying to open your briefcase?" she whispered.

"For spying."

She blinked. "Spying?"

"Don't you play innocent with me."

He should call the cops. Should do it right now and get the matter out of his hands. That's what he should do, but he couldn't quite bring himself to turn her in.

And he hated that she'd put him in this position, hated that he was hesitating, hated that his father's legacy gave him a soft spot for a sweet-looking, devious woman.

"I'm not spying," she repeated.

"Right." He stared down at his telephone, trying to make himself pick it up.

"I'm *not*."

Her eyes looked innocent, and her protest rang sincere, but Dallas wasn't a fool.

"You could get ten years for this," he said harshly, unaccountably angry at her for having put herself in this tenuous position.

Her jaw dropped open and her eyes deepened to turquoise. She looked young, innocent, edgy.

It only made him madder. "Breaking and entering, obstruction of justice—"

"Obstruction of jus—"

Dallas swore. "Tell me about Randy Calloway."

She gave him that confused blink again. "What about Randy?"

"Listen, I'm trying to be a nice guy here, but if you're going to lie to me, I'm calling the cops right now."

She drew back at the phrase "nice guy" and her mouth worked silently for a moment. "What do you want to know about Randy?"

"Everything."

"I met him downstairs."

"When?"

"An hour ago."

"I mean, the first time. Was it before you got the job here? Before you showed up at Allison's?"

There was a knock on the office door, and Allan's voice came through. "Dallas?"

"Yeah?"

"Shelby in there?"

Dallas pressed his fingertips tightly against his forehead. "Yeah. She is."

"Uh..." Allan's voice trailed off, and Dallas swore under his breath. God only knew what Allan was thinking.

"You want me to get Margaret to watch the phones?" asked Allan.

Dallas let out a hard sigh. "Please do."

There was a silent pause. "Okay."

Dallas glared at Shelby. "You see what you've done?"

"What?"

He pointed back and forth between them. "He's going to think we're..."

Her eyes widened. "Why would he think that? Did you tell him—"

"*No!* Of course not. I didn't tell him a thing."

"We'll we're not. We're *so* not."

"Right," Dallas agreed. "Tell me about Randy. When was the first time you met with him?"

Shelby sank down into one of Dallas's guest chairs, supporting herself by leaning on the padded arm. "I told you. An hour ago. In Frappino's."

"Quit lying."

"I'm *not* lying."

Dallas took the other guest chair, trying another tack. "I want to believe you, Shelby. The last thing in the world I want to do is have my partner's fiancée's roommate arrested for obstruction of justice."

"What did I obstruct?"

"Why do you want my briefcase?" The only things in his briefcase were reports on the Perth-Abercrombie case. There was nothing else she could be after.

She froze. "I can't tell you that."

"You *have* to tell me."

She leaned forward. "Why do you think I want your briefcase?"

Dallas hesitated, sizing up her expression. Either she was telling the truth or something was screwing up his litigating instincts. He'd questioned plenty of witnesses, both honest and dishonest. He could always tell the difference—couldn't always prove it, but he always knew.

He decided to push her a little harder. "I think you're leaking evidence to Randy Calloway."

She did the innocent, turquoise blink again. "Evidence on what?"

Maybe she *was* a master con artist.

"Evidence on the Perth-Abercrombie embezzlement case," he said.

"I didn't even know there was a Perth-Abercrombie embezzlement case."

Dallas peered into her eyes, beginning to wonder if she'd been trained by the CIA. There wasn't a single sign of dishonesty. No micro eye movements, no expression changes, not even a single flinch.

"Why did you want my briefcase?"

"I can't tell you that."

"Then I can't trust you."

She bit her lower lip.

The clock ticked off the minutes in the corner of his office.

Standoff.

There was another knock on the door. Allan's voice again. "Shelby?"

"Yes?" Shelby answered.

"Allison is on the phone."

Shelby flinched.

Dallas's eyebrows twitched. Allison was in on it, too? What in the hell was going on here?

"Transfer it in here," Dallas called.

Now Shelby looked frightened. Good.

The phone on the desk rang.

"Speaker phone," said Dallas.

"Not a chance," said Shelby, jumping up.

"You do realize I can have you arrested," he said.

"Arrested isn't convicted," she replied. "And I didn't do anything."

She picked up the phone. "Allison."

While Allison talked, Shelby closed her eyes and sighed.

"He's right here," she said.

Then, "I think so."

Followed by, "Not yet."

"Right.

"Bye." She hung up the phone.

Dallas stared at her in silence. "You going to tell me what's going on, or do I call the cops?"

"I'm not stealing evidence on anything for anyone. That's what's going on."

"Prove it."

"How? You want to call Randy and ask him?"

Dallas coughed out an incredulous laugh. "Right."

"Then how do I prove it? Just tell me. I'll do it."

Dallas thought about that. Only way to prove she wasn't giving away evidence was for her to *not* give away the evidence. Which she wouldn't, now that he'd caught her.

But even if she didn't, it didn't mean she hadn't tried. There really wasn't any way to prove her innocence.

Of course there wasn't any way to prove her guilt, either.

But there was a way to stop her.

"Hearing's on Monday," he said.

She held up her hands in a shrug.

"You stay within my sight until then."

She blinked. Her eyes went from turquoise to jade. "For *two days?*"

"Right. And if Randy calls, you put him on the speaker."

"Two days? And *three* nights?"

"Yes."

"But?"

"Randy goes on the speaker phone."

"I don't care if Randy goes on the speaker phone. You serious about this?"

"Within my sight. Twenty-four hours a day. Take it or leave it."

SHELBY DIDN'T SEE that she had any choice.

The alternative was getting arrested or fired, or possibly both. Besides, if she stayed within Dallas's sight, then he'd have to stay within her sight...along with his briefcase.

And even Dallas would have to sleep at some point. When he did, she'd rescue the pictures. She was pretty sure she'd been making progress on the lock with the bent paperclip when he'd caught her.

Since she wasn't spying, he could hardly catch her giving away evidence.

In fact, the only downside she could see to Plan D was that they might accidentally have sex in the middle of the night. But since she'd sworn off bosses and he'd, apparently, sworn off navels, there wasn't even much danger of that.

Feeling better by the second, she couldn't resist putting a teasing note in her voice. "Your place or mine?"

He rounded the desk and picked up the phone. "Mine. You sit tight while I clear my schedule."

She pointed to the office door. "What about my job?"

"Margaret can cover for the rest of the afternoon."

That was fine with Shelby, but Margaret might not be too thrilled.

Shelby waited in the office while Dallas spent about ten minutes on the phone with his secretary. If she had to have an unrequited crush on somebody, she certainly had good taste.

He really was an incredibly sexy man. He was intelligent, articulate, a little bit demanding, but his voice heated a woman's blood in a way that made the actual words irrelevant.

He hung up the phone and stood up from his chair. "Let's go."

Shelby stood up, glancing at her watch. It was only four o'clock. "Where?"

"There's a cocktail party at Eamon Perth's mansion tonight, and you need a dress."

"So, we're stopping at Allison's place?" Perfect. She could slip Allison some information on Plan D.

"No. We're stopping at Arianne Eastern."

Shelby frowned. "That's an old ladies store."

"We're not going to the place you usually shop."

"What's wrong with DL Clearance Outlets? They have great deals on designer clothes if you're patient."

Dallas let his gaze stray up and down her outfit. "We don't have that kind of time."

"But—"

Dallas held up a hand as he opened the door. And Shelby stopped talking while they crossed the reception area.

"Why can't we just stop at my place and get a dress?" she asked as they headed for the elevators. It seemed like a silly waste of money to buy a new one. Money that Shelby didn't have to spare.

Dallas punched the elevator button. "I've seen your dresses."

"One. You've seen *one* of my dresses."

The door slid open and they stepped into an empty car.

"Two. Plus, I've seen the way you dress all week."

"Right. The navel thing. I'll have you know I have dresses that completely cover my navel."

"This party is at the home of a *very* important client. With other important clients in attendance. You need a respectable dress."

Shelby crossed her arms over her chest. "Excuse me?"

The elevator doors slid open at the lobby. "Respectable," Dallas repeated. "I'm sure you know what the word means."

"Staid and boring, apparently." She matched her pace to his as they headed for the street. "If you make me do this, you're paying."

"Story of my life."

"Well, if you'd let women wear their own clothes—"

"Women? What makes you think I've ever done this before? What makes you think I've ever come across anybody remotely like you before?"

Shelby decided to forgo the character debate. "Respectable," she scoffed.

"As in, I don't want you looking, saying or doing *anything* outrageous."

"You mean, I can't dance on the tables?"

He glared at her as they headed out the glass door to the noise and movement of Lancome Street.

"Swallow the goldfish?" she persisted.

He ignored her.

"Wear a lampshade on my head?"

The only reaction was a tightening of his jaw.

"I can see this isn't going to be any fun at all."

He held up his hand to hail a cab. Then he turned and pointed at her like a schoolteacher. He opened his mouth, then paused.

She stared mulishly up at him while a panel truck whooshed across two lanes to the angry honking of three vehicles.

"Just...don't...have *any* fun," he said.

A grin tried to force its way out, and she turned her bottom lip inside and bit down to stop it.

"Because, if you think it's fun," he continued, "I think we can be damn sure I won't like it."

"Guess I'd better not kiss you again," she said.

A taxi came to a halt, and he shot her a glare as he opened the back door.

"'Cause that was fun," she said as she climbed in.

Dallas slammed the door behind her.

Well, it was.

6

THE DRESSES at Arianne Eastern weren't as bad as Shelby had expected. Dallas's taste, however, was every bit as dull as she'd feared.

He liked full skirts, long sleeves and geometric prints. Shelby wanted a little style, a little pizzazz, a little color, and maybe something more than her ankles and wrists sticking out from miles and miles of fabric. At this rate, she was going to have to change her name to Sister Mary-Agnes.

She headed out of the changing room in a flowing, muumuu-look shirt with bell sleeves, green piping and earth tone swirls over a pair of white palazzo pants.

"This is a joke, right?" she said to Dallas, who was sitting in a leather armchair next to a three-sided mirror. The cream-colored carpet was soft under her bare feet, and a saleslady stood back a discrete distance.

He made a spinning motion with his index finger. "Turn around."

She whirled and the shirt puffed out like a tent.

"Elegant," he said.

She pulled out the front of the top. "And functional. If it rains we can all take shelter under here."

"I like it."

"Forget it." Shelby turned and headed back to the big changing room. The dresses she'd picked covered one wall of the square room. The dresses Dallas had picked covered another.

Her turn this time.

"Take this, Mr. Williams." She popped a perky little silver dress over her head. The high, lace neckline was the only demure thing about it. Sleeveless, it left her shoulders bare. The bodice was tight, a silver lace layer over a silky beige layer, giving the illusion that her skin could be seen in the background. The *very* short skirt puffed out faux ballerina style, showing off her thighs, and making bending over totally out of the question.

She tugged open the change room door and strutted out onto the cushy carpet.

Dallas's eye widened and he sucked in a quick breath.

"You like?" she asked with a waggle of her eyebrows.

"Get serious," he replied.

"I'm perfectly serious."

"You'd go out in public like that?"

"Sure." She worked out. Her thighs were in pretty good shape.

"Vulgar," he said.

"Chic," she responded.

"Next."

Shelby gave a theatrical sigh before turning back.

Dallas's next dress was polka dots. Hundreds of white polka dots on a muddy brown background. The skirt was chiffon, with a satin slip, and the velvet sash was more suited to a little girl than a matriarch. The neckline and sleeves, however, would smoothly cover up any wrinkled skin.

Shelby stomped out.

"You have atrocious taste," she said to Dallas.

"At least you won't get any propositions in that."

"People proposition you if they think you're attractive."

"What? You take propositions as a compliment?"

She glared at her triple image in the mirror. Dowdy didn't begin to describe it. "Don't be absurd. Just because a woman wants to look attractive doesn't mean she's easy."

"These are *conservative* people, Shelby."

"But I doubt they're blind."

He sighed. "All I'm asking for is a little cooperation tonight. I'm the one doing *you* a favor, remember."

"You're doing me a favor? How do you figure?"

"Considering the alternative was having you arrested, I don't think a party is too much of a hardship."

Shelby paused. Fine. All right. She *could* see his perspective.

In his mind, he was doing her a favor. Since she couldn't explain her need for his briefcase, she supposed he was entitled to fill in the blanks by himself.

That didn't mean she was going out in public looking like an overstuffed children's toy.

"Next," she muttered, heading back to the change room.

She searched through the stacks of dresses, genuinely looking for a compromise. She'd chosen a gorgeous, red crepe-look dress, with a tight, strapless bodice and a soft, full skirt that would practically float when she walked. She didn't dare put it on because she knew she'd want to cry when Dallas dismissed it.

She also set aside a flirty, see-through blue silk dress. A hippy-bohemian style, it was slit up the front past the knees, opened to a peek-a-boo midriff that showed off her navel and a whole lot more, and was topped with a bikini-like bodice with a halter strap.

It was gorgeous, fun and flirty. Dallas would hate it on sight.

Then she found it. A simple black sheath. It had sleeves, though they were string lace adorned with hundreds of silver sequins. The bodice cut straight across, so her cleavage wouldn't show. The viscose blend was probably tighter than Dallas would like, but it wasn't spandex. And the only sexy detail was a chain of small, oval, open patches down each side. Those, she'd cover up with her arms while she modeled.

She slipped into the dress and it fit her like a glove. She adjusted the sleeves, so they'd stay closed at the shoulder while she modeled. Under normal circumstances, a slit in the lace would open up so that her shoulders were revealed.

No need to point that little feature out to Dallas up front.

She held her arms by her sides, testing to make sure the openings didn't show.

Hmm.

Not bad.

Demure, yet a kick of style.

She carefully opened the door.

Dallas watched her intently, without saying a word.

She walked as serenely and gracefully as possible, trying to look conservative and respectable—like the kind of person who would never dream of dancing on a table.

"What do you think?" she asked.

He stood up and walked around her. "What do *you* think?"

Shelby made a face, playing it up just a bit. "The hem's kind of long."

"No it's not."

"It's not exactly what I'd pick," she said. "But, I suppose..."

Sensing agreement, the saleslady moved forward. "It fits perfectly," she said with an enthusiastic nod. Her hand started toward Shelby's arm. "Did you notice—"

Shelby quickly stepped away before the woman could point out the openings. "It's pretty expensive," she said to Dallas, as though she really cared.

He waved a dismissive hand, making the saleslady smile.

"And I'm going to need underwear," Shelby added, inching her way toward the changing room.

"On the second floor," said the saleslady.

"And shoes," Shelby added, quickly opening and closing the door before Dallas could look more closely at the dress or have second thoughts.

THE BLACK DRESS wasn't quite as conservative as Dallas had hoped, but at least it didn't raise his blood pressure beyond the danger point the way most of her outfits did. For the rest of the weekend, he was dressing her in sweatpants and oversize T-shirts, so she wouldn't distract him from his work. At least he didn't have to take her out of the apartment after this.

"Shelby?" he called through the bathroom door.

She'd tried to change in his guest room—the one with the conveniently located extension phone. But Dallas wasn't stupid.

"I'm almost ready," she called back.

"We're going to be late."

"Keep your shorts on."

"It's seven-thirty."

"I'm drying my nails."

Dallas tried the locked knob. "You don't need nails."

She carefully opened the door with her flat palms. "You're impossible."

"Dry them on the way."

"Fine. But you have to do up the clasps on my shoes."

Dallas took a step back as she emerged into the hall. He blinked. Then he shook his head to clear his vision. When that didn't work, he squinted.

He could feel his pulse rate inching up. "What *in the hell* did you do to that dress?"

She glanced over her shoulder, looking down the length of the outfit. "What?"

"There are holes in it!" he sputtered. "And the sleeves. You tore the sleeves."

She reached for the dangling icicles of silver sequins that dripped over her bare shoulders. "I didn't do anything to the sleeves."

He stared in stunned silence at the slinky sheath that rippled and hugged its way down her body. He could swear the skirt was shorter. Her soft, caramel skin winked out in a dozen places down each side. If she was wearing underwear under there, it was only barely.

What appeared plain Jane in the store, now looked like the flimsy wrapping of a sultry sex goddess. How the hell had she done it?

"What did you do?" he asked hoarsely.

"I accessorized." She stuffed her feet into spike-heeled black sandals, wiggled one ankle and looked expectantly up at him.

Yeah, like he was going to bend down and play with her legs.

She raised her eyebrows. "I thought you said we were going to be late?"

"We're not going anywhere with you dressed like that."

"You know, some day you're going to make some lucky girl a tyrant of a father."

"You have to change."

"Into *what*? You agreed on the dress. We agreed on the dress. Now, do up my sandals so we can get going."

Dallas gritted his teeth. He had half a mind to leave her behind and go to the party himself. But if she was spying, that might destroy his case, and his chances of impressing Perth-Abercrombie.

Maybe that's what she was counting on. Being left behind to do her dirty work.

Nice try, Shelby.

Dallas crouched down.

She stuck out one foot and a little platinum anklet winked at him. The woman had the sexiest ankles in the world, slim, neat, smooth. Her calves were like burnished silk, and his fingertips grew warm where he contacted her skin.

He didn't dare let his gaze roam to her thighs.

He fumbled with the first delicate clasp, his fingers feeling big and uncoordinated. Who had designed the damn closure, Houdini?

By the time he finally got it right, his blood pressure had nearly doubled.

When she put out her other foot, she lost her balance,

and braced one hand against the top of his head. His gaze caught her thighs and he nearly groaned in agony.

He focused on the shoe, telling himself she couldn't be trusted. She was angling to get left behind. There was no other explanation.

He finished.

Thank God.

And straightened.

"Ready?" He was pretty proud of the neutral tone of his voice.

"As long as you open the doors." She blew gently on her lavender nails. "I'm right behind you. Can you grab my purse?"

Derek picked up the small beaded black bag she'd chosen at Arianne Eastern, and tucked it under her arm. She'd taken her hair down. It glowed in auburn waves, a thick satin curtain caressing her bare shoulders.

Her makeup was perfect. Her eyes were in a dark jade kind of mood. Someday he'd have to figure out what that meant. He was pretty sure turquoise meant she was nervous. Sapphire meant she was angry. Lime meant she was teasing. But so far jade had eluded him.

He turned away from her and opened the door of his apartment, stepping to one side so that she could go first. He steadfastly kept his gaze above her waist.

"So, what's the plan?" she asked as he locked the door.

"Plan?"

"You said there was an important client giving the party. What are we doing? What do you need?"

We? Dallas didn't *think* so. "It's just drinks and casual conversation."

They started down the hall.

"Oh, come on. You canceled everything else on your schedule. You kept this. You bought me a dress. There has to be a reason."

"I'm working on a fraud case for Eamon Perth. As you *already* know."

"Only because you told me."

"Right." Dallas drew out the word.

Shelby stepped inside the waiting elevator. "So, he's this big important client and you want...what from him?"

"His business."

"What else?"

"Nothing."

"So you don't trust your lawyering skills?"

"Why wouldn't I trust my *lawyering* skills?"

"You don't think you're a good enough lawyer to get more of his business, so you're trying to schmooze him. I can respect that. You want me to chat him up?"

"No!"

Shelby shrugged. "I've known a lot of men—"

"I'll just bet you have," Dallas muttered.

"Hey! If my nails weren't still wet, I'd sock you for that. Just because I don't dress like the Queen of England on a dowdy day, doesn't mean I'm slutty."

"I never said you were slutty."

"You don't have to say it when you're thinking it all the time."

"I don't think you're slutty."

"Is this because I kissed you?"

"No." Dallas closed his eyes and gave his head a little shake. He didn't want to think about their kiss. Not when she was standing in front of him looking like his deepest fantasy. Not when she was spending the next three nights in his apartment...

Sweatpants and T-shirts after tonight. There was no other answer.

The elevator came to a stop and he opened his eyes. "I'm sorry. You're right. My remark was uncalled for." He gestured for her to go first.

Her full lips pouted for a second longer, and then she started walking. "All I was going to say was, in my experience, men lose approximately fifty percent of their brain power when they come in contact with any halfway attractive woman. If we work as a tag team, you might be able to use that to your advantage."

"I don't need to *use you to my advantage*. And Eamon Perth is not about to choose his legal counsel based on who's the best flirt."

She shrugged her sexy shoulders. "Hey, I didn't make the rules, I just pay attention to them."

Dallas hit his remote car lock through the glass door at the front of the apartment lobby. "They're a brokerage firm full of professional accountants. I can assure you, they won't lose sight of the bottom line the minute an attractive woman shows up."

Shelby sent him a calculating smile as they crossed the sidewalk to the quiet turnaround drive in front of the apartment. "Oh, yeah?"

"Yeah."

"Men are men."

"What's that supposed to mean?"

"Take you."

He raised his eyebrows in her direction.

"So far, over the course of our relationship, you've spent fifteen bucks on taxi fare, twenty—no *forty*, to bribe the dry cleaner, fifty to get us into Balley's. You paid for the drinks. You spent four hundred on this dress, two-fifty for the shoes, nearly as much for the purse, and one twenty-five for the ankle bracelet."

Dallas couldn't help himself, he glanced down at her ankle.

She slid into the passenger seat of his car. "You're telling me you didn't lose sight of the bottom line?"

"Not in the least." Though he sure hadn't quantified it in those terms before.

"Right." She pulled her sexy ankles inside. "And so far you got what? A kiss? It wasn't even that great a kiss."

He almost defended the quality of the kiss, but he quickly stopped himself.

"You mean to tell me," she continued into his silence, "if I was sixty-five, with sallow skin and hair on my upper lip, you'd have done the same thing?"

"Your argument is illogical," said Dallas, quickly closing her door.

"It's perfectly logical," she picked up as he climbed in the driver's side. "Besides, all I'm trying to do is help you."

He turned the ignition. "Can we rewind here? I've forgotten exactly how it is you're trying to *help* me. Guess maybe I got stuck back there where you were spying on me."

"You know I'm not spying on you."

He put the car into gear and checked his mirrors. "Come again?"

"If you really thought I was spying on you, you'd have called the cops." She pulled back in her seat as he accelerated out of the parking spot and into traffic.

"Thirty seconds ago, you said I'd kept you around because you weren't sixty-five with hair on your upper lip. Which is it?"

"I've got both of those things going for me."

He slowed down for a light, shooting her an incredulous look.

"Hey, like I said, I didn't make the rules. Now. What's the plan? What are you trying to get from Eamon Perth, and how can I help?"

"You can help by keeping quiet and staying still."

"That's not very challenging."

The light turned green and Dallas smirked as he accelerated and shifted into second. "For you? Oh, yeah. It is."

DALLAS HAD ONLY BEEN to Eamon Perth's home on one other occasion. The classic, Italianate mansion had impressed him then, and it impressed him now. From the gold-leaf grandfather clock and the carved cherrywood railing that graced the palatial foyer, to the ivory silk armchairs in the living room and the Grecian-pillared three-story atrium in the center, the Perths had created an oasis of comfort and elegance.

Tonight, the party guests spilled from the foyer to the living room and dining room, and into the atrium beyond.

"Dallas." Eamon held out his hand where he was greeting guests in the foyer. "So glad you could make it. You remember my wife, Pamela?"

Dallas let go of Eamon's hand and shifted his attention. "Very nice to see you again, Pamela. Thank you so much for the invitation."

Pamela smiled, and her gaze moved to Shelby.

Dallas stepped back with a quick prayer and a fervent hope for the best. "This is my friend, Shelby Jacobs."

"Nice to meet you both," said Shelby, shaking each of their hands in turn.

Dallas let out his breath. So far, so good. And, although Pamela was wearing a floor-length gown, Shelby's dress didn't seem too far out of place. A little shorter than most, and he got nervous whenever she moved her hands away from her sides and flashed her skin, but there were plenty of other women in cocktail dresses.

Eamon gazed quizzically at Shelby. "Have we met before?"

Shelby cocked her head. "I don't know. Have you ever been to Minneapolis?"

Eamon nodded. "I usually get there a couple of times a year."

"Really? Ever been to the Terra Suma Cocktail Lounge?"

Eamon stilled, a look of alarm creeping into his eyes.

Dallas reached for Shelby's arm to shut her up.

Not fast enough.

"I used to be a cocktail waitress there," she offered.

"You did?" asked Pamela, sliding a disapproving glance her husband's way.

Dallas wished the floor would open up and swallow him. Better yet, he wished it would open up and swallow Shelby. And hold her there—without a telephone until the party was over.

"I don't believe I've ever been there," said Eamon.

Dallas prayed she wouldn't press it.

To his relief, she shrugged. "I'm sure I would have

remembered you if you had. You must have me mixed up with someone else."

Eamon visibly sighed. Okay, Dallas would give her points for that save.

"You were a *cocktail* waitress?" asked Pamela, obviously not about to let the Minneapolis connection die a quick and merciful death.

Shelby hesitated for a split second. "Part-time. In college. I went to U. of M."

Pamela perked up. "My sister went to U. of M. What was your major?"

"Philosophy."

"Oh." Pamela nodded politely, the animation leaving her expression. "Philosophy."

"With a minor in economics," said Shelby.

That perked Pamela back up.

"She's doing client relations now," said Dallas.

Shelby flashed him a look of surprise, but went along with the exaggeration. "That's how I met Dallas."

Pamela's gaze flitted past Dallas's ear, her attention momentarily distracted. She leaned toward her husband. "Eamon," she muttered under her breath, nodding toward the door behind them.

Dallas was too polite to look. But Shelby, having no such compunction, turned to stare at the front door.

"I'll take care of it," said Eamon.

"Daddy," came a high voice behind them.

Dallas turned to see a young woman of about twenty saunter across the burgundy area rug in what looked like spun pink Saran wrap. Her blond hair was teased to add about four inches at her head, and her high, strapless sandals added four inches at her feet. Huge beaded earrings dangled to her bare shoulders. Her makeup was bright, her lashes enormous.

She made Shelby look sedate by comparison, and Dallas was overjoyed.

"Sorry I'm late," she pouted as she joined the group.

"Courtney," said Pamela in an admonishing voice. "This is Dallas Williams and Shelby Jacobs. Dallas, Shelby, this is our daughter, Courtney."

"Nice to meet you, Courtney," said Dallas, growing uncomfortable at the vibes running between the three, and looking to make a hasty escape.

"*Great dress*," said Shelby, apparently oblivious to the tension. She stepped forward to shake Courtney's hand. "A Varian?"

Courtney struck a pose. "Got it in Paris last week."

"Excellent," said Shelby, looking her up and down. "I wasn't crazy about all that retro stuff in her spring collection, but looks like she's gone minimalist for fall."

Courtney nodded. "You see the Asian-inspired jackets?"

Shelby shook her head. "Not yet."

"Raw silk, mandarin collars, a sort of origami fold thing goin' on. And the colors are to die for."

Shelby held out her open palms with an apologetic frown. "Got this one at Arianne Eastern."

Courtney made a face. "My *mom* shops there."

Dallas's gaze flew to Pamela's expression, and he froze in dread.

"I don't think you can beat it for class and sophistication," said Shelby smoothly, turning to include Pamela in the conversation. "Dallas picked out a gorgeous gold silk-chiffon gown there this afternoon, but I just couldn't pull it off."

Pamela smiled, apparently ready to accept Shelby's second save of the evening. Dallas felt like he was dodging bullets.

"Wanna go get some shooters?" Courtney asked Shelby, nodding toward a bar in the corner of the spacious living room.

"Sure," Shelby quickly agreed, and the two scampered off like new best friends.

Eamon cleared his throat. "Well, Dallas. She seems...nice."

"Thank you," said Dallas, not sure whether to be relieved or terrified that Shelby and Courtney had left to have shooters. "We're just friends."

Eamon extended his arm and gestured toward the door. "Ah, I see Hal Webber's arrived. I'd like to introduce the two of you. He's the manager of the Hawthorn Club. Remember we talked about getting you a recommendation for membership?"

"I do," said Dallas, nodding in easy agreement, relieved to discover Shelby's antics hadn't completely blown him out of the water with Eamon.

After talking to Hal, Dallas moved from conversation group to conversation group, keeping a close watch on Shelby. Luckily, she and Courtney were staying still. Unfortunately, they were staying still at the bar, downing shooters at an alarming rate, and drawing a crowd.

A small band had started up in the far corner of the atrium, and several of the guests were dancing under the stars. Through an open set of double doors, balls clacked in the billiard room, and a sumptuous buffet was set up in the dining room.

As the evening wore on, Shelby and Courtney's laughter grew louder, and their skirts shifted higher.

Perched cross-legged on a little bar stool, Shelby tipped her head back and laughed at something Courtney had said. Her white teeth flashed and her eyes lit up. Then she wriggled forward to talk, and Dallas found himself shifting closer, straining to hear her voice.

His gaze moved from her shimmering hair to her smooth shoulders, down the inch-wide oval cutouts along the sides of her dress—the golden skin beside her breast, the smooth glimpse of her hips, and a flash of golden thigh. He followed her impossibly long legs to the black high-heeled sandals he'd fastened earlier.

His fingers tingled as he remembered cradling her ankle. His pulse jumped as he remembered the scent of her skin. The rest of he crowd faded to the background and he moved closer still.

She was talking, holding an impromptu audience of Eamon's associates to rapt attention. "So, a guy walks into a bar with a monkey on his shoulder, and says 'a beer for me, and three for the monkey.'"

Holy crap!

Dallas knew the punch line to that one.

He rushed forward and grasped Shelby's hand.

"Hey, Dallas." She gave him a sloppy grin. "How's it going?"

"Let's dance." He tugged her from the stool.

"Great idea! Whoops." She stumbled in her heels, grabbing Courtney's hand on the way by. "Come on, Courtney. Dallas wants to dance!"

He was in the middle of the dance floor, trying in vain to ignore Shelby's sinewy, sensuous body as she gyrated to a vintage Beatles song, when he realized *both* women were dancing with him. Arms in the air, eyes closed, Courtney swayed to the beat, hip-bumping with Shelby and creating a threesome.

Dallas glanced around in horror, groaning inwardly as he caught the reproachful expression in Eamon's eyes.

Who could blame the man? Dallas would be pissed, too, if he caught somebody in the middle of a ménage à trois with his daughter, in his atrium, in front of fifty of his most important friends and colleagues.

He tried to back away—but Shelby caught his hand.

Eamon squinted, and for the second time since he'd met Shelby, Dallas wished somebody would just shoot him.

7

SHELBY STRETCHED her tired limbs against the soft leather of Dallas's front seat as the streetlights strobed shadows across the dashboard and classical music throbbed from the hidden speakers.

"Great party," she sighed, the shooters wearing off to a pleasant buzz. She'd been surprised at how much fun she'd had.

He jammed the gearshift into third, chirping the tires on the dry asphalt. "I cannot *believe* you did that."

"Did what?"

"Managed to undo in one party what it's taken me six months to build."

Now that threw her for a loop. She thought it had gone extremely well. She hadn't flirted with anybody. She'd had fun with Eamon's daughter, stayed out of Dallas's way. "What did I do?"

"Your behavior was reprehensible."

"Whoa. Because I laughed?"

"Way too loud."

She ignored that. "Because I danced?"

"With *Courtney*."

"Because I had a couple of drinks?"

"Six."

"Or maybe you're mad because I lied for you."

He shot a glance across the front seat. "Lied for me?"

"*Client relations?*" she asked.

He had the good grace to look embarrassed. "It was merely semantics."

"Well, the rest of it was a whole lot more than semantics, because I never took a single economics course. I worked *full-time* as a cocktail waitress, and not just when I was in college. I only quit two weeks ago. And yes, Eamon Perth has been to the Terra Suma Cocktail Lounge in Minneapolis."

"You were a *cocktail waitress* until two weeks ago?"

"Right."

"Allison told Greg you were experienced."

"I am. He just never asked what the experience was in."

"I don't believe this."

"You don't want to know who Eamon Perth was at the Terra Suma with?"

Dallas shook his head and careened around a corner. "None of my business."

Shelby reached for the handle above the door and hung on. "Now, me, I'd be curious."

"You already know who he was with."

"I meant if I was you."

Dallas pulled onto the street in front of his apartment building. "Well, I'm not like you. I don't need to know the seamy side of people's lives."

"Anybody ever tell you you're kind of boring?"

He zipped into a parking spot and pulled the hand brake. "Anybody ever tell you you're kind of nosy?"

"Anybody ever tell you you're kind of sexy?"

His eyes went wide and he made a strangled sound in the back of his throat.

"Sorry," she said. "That just kind of popped out."

"Well, *pop it* back in."

"Right."

He opened his door and she followed suit.

"I have to call Allison," she said as they crossed the sidewalk and Dallas hit the remote car door lock.

"Forget it."

"If I don't, she's going to worry." About more than Shelby's whereabouts.

"Should have thought of that before you started spying."

"Haven't we had this conversation before?"

He inserted his key and opened the oversize glass door that led to a spacious lobby. "How do I know you're not going to leak something to her?"

"Oh, right. I forgot. We're a spy ring. She got engaged to Greg two months ago in order to get me into the firm, so I could steal evidence on a case that none of you had even heard of back then. It was a simple plan. Though arranging my arrest, and knowing exactly when you'd show up at the Haines Street lockup to bail me out was a bit tricky. We're amazed you fell for it."

"Quit being sarcastic."

"Quit being unreasonable."

"Fine. But you use the speaker phone this time."

"No."

He punched the elevator button. "What do you mean *no?* I'm calling the shots."

"Oh, you are not. I'm humoring you."

"I don't think—"

"You can listen to my end of the conversation. Not Allison's."

They stepped into the elevator.

Dallas fumed silently, which Shelby took as agreement.

The floor number pinged and the doors slid open.

He gestured for her to go first, expression relaxing for the first time in hours. "I can't believe you were going to tell them the monkey joke."

"It's funny."

"It's disgusting."

"You should have heard the one Courtney told first."

He opened his apartment door. "I do *not* want to know this."

"Lighten up. A little curiosity is good for your health."

He closed the door behind him, hitting a couple of switches. An overhead light came on in the foyer, and gentle pot lights over the fireplace gave the living room a soft glow. "Make your call, and let's get to bed."

Shelby shot him a playful smile. "You may want to rephrase that."

He shook his head and grimaced. "Make the call."

She headed for the telephone in the dimly lit living room, composing in her head. She couldn't report to Allison she'd been successful yet. But success couldn't be too long in coming. It was nearly midnight, and Dallas didn't strike her as a wee hours party animal.

She punched in Allison's number. "Why don't we have a brandy?" she asked Dallas.

"You want more to drink?"

The ring tone buzzed in her ear. "Yeah. Join me." She could nurse her own. But the more he drank, the sooner he'd sleep.

"Shelby?" came Allison's breathless voice.

"Yeah. It's me."

"Where *are you*?"

"I'm with Dallas. Sorry I couldn't call earlier."

"Did you get them?"

Shelby glanced at Dallas's suspicious scowl. Her bizarre joke about having cooked up a master spy scheme with Allison obviously hadn't quelled his suspicions.

"Not yet," she said to Allison.

"What do you mean, not yet?"

"I mean, I haven't had a chance."

"He's going to open the briefcase. He's going to open it and see the pictures."

"Don't worry."

"How can I not worry?"

"I have an idea."

Dallas's eyes narrowed.

"Tell me your idea," Allison demanded.

"Uh, I can't really talk right now."

"Why not?"

"Guess."

"He's there?"

"Right."

"Hang up," said Dallas.

She gave him an annoyed stare. "I gotta go."

"But—"

"I'll call you."

"Shelby—"

Dallas reached forward and lifted the phone out of her hand, then pressed the end button.

"I wish you hadn't done that," said Shelby.

"What's going on?"

"I can't tell you that." She headed for the bar. If he wasn't going to pour the brandy, she was.

He followed behind her, up close, his tone menacing. "I don't know what you two are—"

She turned to face him, holding out a snifter of brandy. "You're paranoid."

He ignored the glass. "Paranoid?"

"Yes."

"Fact. You stole my briefcase."

She held his glass out further. "Borrowed."

He still ignored it. "Fact. You tried to break into my briefcase."

She wiggled her wrist, sloshing the amber liquid in the oversize glass. "Speculation."

"Fact. You have a relationship with Randy Calloway."

"One coffee. Will you take the damn drink."

He glared at the brandy, but took it from her hand. "I don't think you understand exactly what is at stake for me on this."

She stared at him openly, putting every scrap of honesty she could muster into her expression. "Nothing I've done will have any impact on your case for Perth-Abercrombie."

"Problem is," he drawled, taking a swallow of the brandy. "I can't afford to believe that."

"Believe it."

He slowly shook his head. "Not a chance. You have thirty seconds to tell me exactly what's going on here, or I'm calling Allan and Greg and we're firing you tonight."

"You can't call Greg." Shelby wasn't convinced that Plan D was going to fail. She could still FedEx the pictures in time to torture Greg for three days.

"Twenty seconds."

"You don't need to know this."

He moved toward the phone. "Ten."

"I'm telling you the truth."

He picked up the receiver. "Five."

"Dallas."

He pressed a button. "Two."

Shelby swore out loud.

"Time's up."

She huffed out a breath. "Fine. But you have to promise me something."

"You're not in a position to bargain."

"Make me a promise, or make the damn phone call."

Dallas hesitated. Then he set down the phone and eased onto the couch, stretching his legs out in front of him. "Start talking."

Shelby sank down into an oversize armchair, grateful for the brandy. "If I tell you what's going on, you have to promise me, I mean *swear to me*, that you will never, *ever*, on pain of *death*, let Allison know I told you. And you will absolutely, under *no* circumstances, look at what I tell you not to look at."

Dallas blinked. "You've got to be kidding."

She shook her head. "That's the deal. Take it or leave it."

"What are you going to tell me not to look at?"

"Uh-uh. Not until you promise."

His eyes narrowed. His lips pursed. He took a slow, silent drink of his brandy. "Okay."

"You agree?"

He nodded. "I agree."

Shelby took a deep breath. Okay. Plan E. She'd tell Dallas what was going on. He'd hand over the pictures, keep the secret, and she'd hit an all-night courier on her way home.

It could work.

He swirled the brandy in the deep glass, his expression thoughtful, the dim light reflecting off the planes and angles of his face. His shoulders were broad beneath his expensive suit, and he carried himself with an assured air of self-confidence.

For an aggravating man, he certainly was sexy.

"Let's hear it," he prompted.

Shelby steeled herself. "I need something out of your briefcase."

"I *had* figured out that part out already."

"It belongs to Allison."

That got an expression of surprise out of him. "How'd it get in my briefcase?"

"I put it there."

"When?"

"This afternoon. Greg was in the boardroom. So was your briefcase." She shrugged. "I presumed..."

"Wrongly."

"Wrongly."

"What is it?"

She stared at him for a long moment. This was it. The point of no return. "Pictures of Allison."

He drew back, eyebrows arching. "You went through all *this* over pictures of Allison?"

Shelby leaned slightly forward, gazing at him out of the tops of her eyes. "Pictures..." she said. "Of Allison.... That I secretly snuck into Greg's briefcase..."

"What? She's having an affair?"

"*No!* They were..." Shelby gave him her best sultry, come-hither look. "Pictures."

Dallas's mouth dropped open a notch. *"Pictures?"*

Shelby had to stifle a grin. "Of Allison."

"In *my* briefcase?"

"I have been trying to steal them back from you for *twelve* hours."

Dallas set down his brandy glass on the end table with a snap and rocked to his feet. He left the room, returning quickly with his briefcase.

When he undid the locks, Shelby breathed a sigh of relief. Finally. Plan E was going to work.

He opened the lid.

"Two files down," she said.

Dallas slipped out the manila envelope.

He held it up to the light, chuckled and shook his head. "I never would have thought Allison had it in her."

"I talked her into it."

"Why does that not surprise me?"

"You can *not* let on that you know. She'd be mortified."

He fanned the envelope back and forth, meeting Shelby's eyes. "You went through all this to help a friend?"

"I did get her into the mess."

He stared at her for a long minute, as though he'd never seen her before. Then his eyes softened and she felt the warmth of it shimmer through her body.

"You surprise me, Shelby Jacobs," he nearly whispered.

She stood up and crossed the floor. "I surprise myself all the time." She reached for the envelope.

He jerked it back out of her reach and his eyes lit up with trouble.

"Hey!" Shelby nearly overbalanced.

"You must admit," he mused. "This situation is rife with extraordinary possibilities."

"Like what?"

"Like a chance to get to know Allison in a way—"

"I thought you said you weren't interested in the seamy side of other people's lives."

"I've changed my mind. You must be a bad influence."

She glared at him, trying to decide if he was joking or if she'd totally misjudged him. "We had a deal."

"Did you get it in writing?"

"Don't be absurd."

"Next time, you might want to consult a lawyer."

"Hand them over."

"Turns out the item we spoke of earlier is more valuable than I thought."

"You're *not* going to look at them." She couldn't have been that far wrong about him.

"I'm not?"

She shook her head. "Nope."

"A sexy woman...wearing..." He lifted the loose flap on the envelope. "Let's see."

She reached, but his arms were too long. "That's not funny, Dallas."

"Who's trying to be funny? I have in my possession sexy pictures of a beautiful woman. I don't think I should give them up for nothing."

That threw Shelby. "You're trying to *bribe* me?"

"But if," Dallas continued as if she hadn't spoken, "somebody was to replace said sexy pictures with something of equivalent, uh, value, I might be talked into giving them up without looking at them."

Shelby stilled, staring into his eyes. There was no mistaking the dare he'd tossed out. Was he joking? Trying to get a rise out of her?

"Dallas."

"Yeah?"

"You don't want to play this game."

He stared back levelly. "Don't I?"

"Hand over the pictures."

"Give me a pose."

Did she argue further? Call his bluff? Walk out and hope he had enough honor to leave the envelope closed?

If she walked out, she wouldn't be able to honestly tell Allison that she'd retrieved the pictures. And Allison would spend the rest of her life worrying. Shelby had gotten her friend mixed up in this, and it was up to her to get her out.

Besides, she had more guts than Dallas. She gave him all of two minutes before he cried uncle.

She took a few steps away from him, stretching her arms out across the painted mantel and tossing her hair back over her shoulders. She licked her lips, and zeroed in on his gaze.

His eyes widened slightly, and an avalanche of desire rolled through her. "You mean, like this?" Her voice turned bedroom husky.

He shifted in his seat. "You can do better than that."

She hiked her skirt up over one thigh, bending her knee, surprised by her hormonal reaction to the faux striptease. Her pulse sped up, and her mouth went dry. "This?"

"I have a feeling Allison showed a little more skin."

Shelby smirked, taking a couple of steps forward. "Are we talking navel here?"

Dallas was obviously fighting a grin. Who knew the

man could be playful? "We're definitely talking navel," he said.

Playful or not, she was still convinced he'd crack. Might as well speed things up. She reached around her back and slid down the zipper, snaking her arms free and letting the dress slither over her black bra to pool at her hips.

"Better?" she asked, moving closer.

"Getting there," said Dallas, the raw interest in his eyes urging her onward. The envelope slipped out of his hand onto the couch.

"You want more?" she asked.

"You willing to give it?"

She was pretty sure he'd cough up the pictures anytime, but she was curious to see how far he'd go with this.

She gave her dress a final tug, and it slithered over her legs.

His gazed fixed on her lacy bra and her black, high-cut lace panties. The lust in his eyes turned naked and completely uncensored.

Shelby stepped out of the puddle of her dress and moved even closer, within touching distance. She glanced at his broad hands, itchy to have them caress her skin, remembering his touch, remembering his kiss, her nerves growing hot in anticipation. She'd never felt this sexy in her life.

"More?" she breathed, praying he'd say yes.

He didn't answer.

She leaned down and dipped her index finger into his brandy, then she slipped it into her mouth, savoring the heady sweet flavor.

He watched her movements, mesmerized.

Her lungs labored, trying to feed enough oxygen to her body. She forgot about the pictures, forgot about Allison, her job, the party... All she knew was that she was standing in front of the sexiest man on the planet, and she wanted him bad.

She crouched to her knees, so they were face-to-face. "More?" she asked again.

"Yeah," he growled.

She reached around to the clasp of her bra, knowing there'd be no turning back. A woman could flash her thigh and expect a man to walk away. But she didn't bare her breasts unless she was serious.

She clicked the clasp, then positioned one forearm across herself, using the other hand to slide her bra away.

Dallas clenched his fists, his jaw was tight with control. "The pictures are yours," he said.

She didn't move. "I know."

Slowly, obviously giving her ample time to stop him, Dallas reached forward. He touched her arm, gently drawing it away from her chest.

She let it go easily, and he sucked in a breath as he stared at her bare breasts in the golden light.

Then he switched his gaze to her face, and his hand moved behind her neck, cupping her scalp. He moved toward her, pulling her to him.

Her body nearly convulsed with anticipation.

Then their lips joined, and a brandy fire leaped between them.

Dallas levered himself off the couch, kneeling in front of her. His arms went around her, pulling her tight. His suit jacket abraded her nipples, and his mouth heated her lips, her skin, the very core of her being.

The tension of the evening fused them. The tension of the past week anchored them. She saw it clearly now, every argument, every frustration, every tense moment, had been foreplay. They needed a sexual catharsis to clear the air between them.

Dallas must have recognized that, too.

He pulled back, lifted a hand and smoothed her hair from her forehead, stared deeply into her eyes. "We're going to do this?" he asked.

She nodded. "Kind of ironic that this is Plan F."

"Plan F?"

"I'll tell you later."

"Later," he agreed, kissing her again, strumming one thumb across her nipple, sending shock waves along her system.

She pushed his jacket off his shoulders, and he shrugged out of it. Then his attention turned to her neck, planting hot, moist kisses in every sensitive spot.

She struggled with his tie, but had trouble keeping her concentration.

He rolled her panties down, grasping her bare buttocks, his fingers brushing the sensitive skin on her inner thigh.

"You're gorgeous," he breathed. "Stunning."

She felt her body subconsciously strain toward his hands. She'd never had arousal rush at her this fast.

"I can't get your tie undone," she moaned.

He chuckled roughly in her ear, reaching to help her, his strong hand covering hers, working at the knot.

"You're gorgeous, too," she whispered.

"You haven't seen me yet."

"It's not because I'm not trying."

He chuckled again, pulling off his tie. "There."

"Lose the shirt."

"Yes, ma'am." His hands went for the buttons.

"Hey, I like that. Why aren't you always this easy to get along with?"

"Why aren't you always this naked?"

"That solve the problem?" she asked.

"Absolutely." He stripped off his shirt.

Shelby's mouth all but watered as she took in his strong pecs, washboard stomach and broad, bare shoulders. "I doubt we'd get any work done."

"We definitely wouldn't get any work done." He put his arms around her, supporting her spine, as he eased her down onto the plush carpet. Then he pulled back to let his hot gaze take in the length of her naked body. "But I wouldn't care."

"Your partners might."

He slid one hand from the curve of her hip up the side of her rib cage, along the swell of her breast. "I've been wanting to do that all night long."

"So the dress wasn't a total bust?"

He shook his head. When his hand reached her underarm, he kept going, pushing her arm above her head.

"Stunning," he whispered, dipping his head to take her nipple into his mouth.

As his tongue hit her sensitive flesh, a moan leaped from her mouth, and her spine arched in ecstasy.

He pulled back with a masculine smile of satisfaction. "Too bad there isn't something I want to get from you."

She cocked her head. "I thought there *was* something you wanted from me."

"You're a tease."

"Is that a problem?"

"Absolutely not." He reached to the table behind him and lifted his brandy glass. "Sex should be fun." He dipped his own finger into the amber liquid this time, then he moistened her lips with the liquor.

She barely had time to taste the tip of his finger, when he was kissing the brandy away. She lifted her head, opened her mouth, kissed him deeper and deeper.

Too soon, he pulled away, and she drew in rapid breaths.

He dipped his finger again. This time moistening her nipples before thoroughly devouring the sweet brandy.

The sensation was exquisite, and just when she thought she couldn't take another second, he pulled back. She bit down on another moan.

He lifted the glass, trickling a few drops of liquid into her navel.

She watched, mesmerized while he tongued it away, gently flicking the gold ring, expanding his circle of kisses to her entire stomach until she gasped his name.

He pulled back again.

No. No. She hadn't meant stop.

"You okay?" he asked.

"*Yessss.*"

He gave her a sexy, knowing grin. Lifting the glass snifter. This time he trickled the lukewarm liquid over her soft curls.

She nearly came up off the floor when it trickled over her super-sensitive flesh.

He kissed her, and she hissed his name.

He kept kissing, and she reached for his hair as her blood reached the boiling point and sensation began to throb its way up from her toes.

"Dallas."

"Enough?"

"Oh, God."

He pulled back, stroking his rough fingertips along the insides of her thighs.

She spread wider.

"Gorgeous," he whispered, shucking his pants.

"Now," she pleaded, squirming, stuck on an intense plane of arousal.

He positioned himself over her, kissing his way up her abdomen, pausing on each breast as she grasped his back, urging him on, panting in anticipation.

He kissed her neck.

She arched toward him, kissing his temple, digging her nails into the skin of his back.

"You're killing me," she whispered.

"I'm killing myself."

She told him succinctly and crudely just exactly what she wanted him to do and when she wanted him to do it. Which was *now*.

That did it.

He was inside her.

Her nerve endings swelled around him. She arched up as he stroked her. He dipped his fingertip into the brandy once more, covering her lips with the sticky liquid, pushing his finger into the cavern of her mouth so she could tongue the sweet liquid.

Then he replaced his finger with his mouth. His tongue pushed inside, mimicking the movements of his body, taking her to impossible heights.

She locked her ankles around him. "Dallas. Dallas. Dallas."

"Oh, Shelby. I can't... I've never..."

She groaned and her entire body convulsed in a sheet of light.

Dallas was seconds behind her, holding her tight, kissing her hard, his sweat-slicked body pressed against her as if he'd never let go.

8

DALLAS CRADLED SHELBY in his arms amid a disarray of scattered clothes, file folders and a tipped brandy snifter, while he waited for the world to right itself.

She shifted, her warm, damp body rubbing pleasantly against his. "You do realize this has to be a one-shot deal."

"Of course," he muttered against her hair, inhaling its scent, unable to find the energy to make plans past the next five minutes or so.

"I don't do bosses."

He chuckled his disbelief.

She nudged him with her hip. "You know what I mean. And I am definitely not your type."

She was right, of course. His type was about as far away from Shelby as a woman could get. Which made him wonder for a second why he'd never had such mind-blowing sex with someone who *was* his type. But he was too tired to ponder something that complex, so he shelved the question for now.

He shifted, so that her rear end nestled against his stomach, spoon fashion. He kissed the back of her neck, nuzzling the fine hairs at the base of her skull. "If we don't stop, does it still count as one shot?"

She tipped her head, to better expose her neck to his kisses. "I like the way you think, Williams."

"I like the way you taste, Jacobs."

"It's the brandy."

"Uh-uh. It's you."

Her body stiffened as she seemed to suddenly remember something. "You sipped brandy from my navel."

"Yeah?"

"But, you seem so..."

He didn't let the conversation keep him from kissing her, moving from her neck along her shoulder, wondering how long he had to reasonably wait before making love to her again. "I seem so...what?"

"So, I don't know... Staid, conservative, serious."

"Serious guys can't like sex?"

"I expected..."

He stroked the backs of his knuckles over the side of her breast and along the indentation of her waist. "What? Closed-mouth kissing and the missionary position?"

"Something like that."

He chuckled, tugging gently at her ear with his teeth. "Disappointed?"

"Nope."

He waited for a second. "*Nope?* After all that, a nope is the only compliment I get?

She didn't answer, just smirked at the insecurity in his question.

He sighed heavily and touched his forehead to her temple. "You're hard on a guy's ego, you know that?"

She turned onto her back and stared up at him, eyes turning dark jade, expression serious. "How's this? I just had the greatest, most mind-blowing sex of my life, with a guy that surprised the hell out of me."

Dallas's heartbeat thudded deeply in his chest.

"And, I'm wondering," she continued, "how I'm going to face him day in, day out at the office, knowing we can never do it again."

"I withdraw my complaint," he whispered, dipping to capture her mouth in a kiss that was as tender as it was sexy.

Her arms snaked around his neck, and he eased his weight down on top of her. The kiss grew hotter and deeper, and his hands roamed her slick, scented body. "This still counts as once, right?"

"It's once until we stop," she confirmed.

"Perfect." Maybe they'd never stop. Maybe he could keep her here in his apartment for the next six months.

The passion rose quickly between them, and Dallas moved Shelby on top. He didn't want her to think he was overusing the missionary position.

Afterward, he carried her to his bed and tucked a down-filled comforter over them both.

She sighed as she slid into his arms.

"Good?" he asked.

"Good," she agreed.

"So, what's Plan F?"

He felt her vibrate with a laugh. "Plan F is where I have sex with you until you fall asleep and then FedEx the pictures to Greg."

"I like Plan F."

"Thank goodness for that. Plans A through E didn't work out so well."

"Except for the sleeping part. If I call FedEx, can we keep going?"

"They'll pick up in the middle of the night?"

"As long as we're willing to pay." He paused. "Heck,

I'll even spring for the extra fifty-nine, ninety-five, since I got a whole lot more than one lousy kiss this time."

She drew back, lifting the covers slightly and whooshing in a burst of cool air. "*That* was only worth fifty-nine, ninety-five?"

Dallas cringed and groaned out a cussword.

Shelby laughed. "Why don't we count the dress and the jewelry and the purse. Then, you know, I don't have to be insulted."

He reached across the bed and lifted the phone. "I do like the way you think."

WHEN DALLAS GOT BACK from giving the FedEx courier Allison's pictures, Shelby was on the phone with her back to the bedroom door. Since it was nearly three in the morning, he assumed she was talking to Allison.

"What do you mean, I sound funny?"

He paused before entering the room.

"Because it took a while to get them, that's why," she said.

She paused and twisted the phone cord in her fingers. "Because..."

Another pause.

"Okay. Yeah. I did."

She let go of the cord and raked her fingers through her messy hair. "Because I had to distract him *somehow*."

Dallas's ego pinched on that one.

"It was fine."

Fine?

"Don't worry about it."

He made a show of banging against the door as he walked into the room.

She turned to look at him and smiled, and he put a possessive hand on her shoulder. He had no right to be upset about her motives. She'd taken him to heaven and back, twice.

He kissed the top of her head.

And that had to be enough.

"I'll see you in the morning," she said to Allison. "Now *sleep*."

She put her hand over Dallas's. "Okay. Goodbye."

He climbed back into bed beside her. "She's good?"

Shelby nodded. "She's good." She gave a heavy sigh. "Thank goodness that's over with."

Dallas felt the same way. It was an enormous sense of relief to discover Shelby wasn't a criminal. The thought of being forced to call the cops on her had eaten away at him all evening long. But she was innocent. There was a logical explanation for everything.

He stilled.

Wait a minute.

Not *quite* everything.

"Tell me about Randy Calloway," he said softly.

"Jealous?" she asked, a trace of laughter deep in her throat.

"No." Maybe a little. "Suspicious."

"I told you, I barely know him."

"Tell me again. How did you meet him?"

"This morning. I mean, yesterday, in Frappino's."

"You approach him, or did he approach you?"

"He approached me. It was crowded, and he wanted to sit in my extra chair."

"What did he talk about?"

Shelby grinned and tipped her head to look at Dallas's face. "He wants to date me. I know this may shock and surprise you, but some men find me attractive."

"Got news for you, Jacobs. *All* men find you attractive."

"Yeah, right."

He didn't argue the point, and he resisted the urge to ask her if she'd said yes to the date. "Did he talk about anything else?"

She thought for a moment. "He knew I worked on the eighth floor."

"And?"

"At one point he asked me if I worked for any particular lawyer."

All of Dallas's senses went on alert. This was definitely no coincidence. "Could you see him again?"

"I'm meeting him for coffee on Monday."

So she *had* said yes to the date. Dallas tamped down a spike of jealousy. "Shelby?"

"What?"

"I need to ask you to do something for me."

Her eyebrows went up in a question mark.

"Spy on Randy Calloway."

Her forehead furrowed. "Let me get this straight. Spying on you was going to get me jail time, but now you *want* me to spy on Randy?"

"I think Randy's trying to spy on me."

She popped her head up. "Counterespionage?"

"Nothing that dramatic." He pulled her back down on his shoulder where it felt like she belonged. "Just meet him, see what he says. If I'm right, he'll ask you to give him some information from the office. Can you play dumb?"

She widened her eyes and blinked ingenuously.

"God, you're beautiful," said Dallas.

"Who? Li'l ol' me? Why, I'm just a receptionist cocktail waitress."

Dallas chuckled. "I said dumb, not Scarlet O'Hara."

She laughed softly, her eyes fluttering closed. Then the laughter died away and her features relaxed, her cheek going soft against him.

He waited, but she didn't open her eyes.

"Sleep," Dallas whispered.

She breathed a deep sigh.

He twisted his head to kiss her lips one more time, tasting the bittersweet flavor of brandy and goodbye.

ALLISON HIT the blender's off button, her banana breakfast shake settling into the bottom of the glass pitcher as her eyes went wide and her voice rose higher. "You *FedExed* them?"

Shelby nodded.

"I thought you were going to bring them *home.*"

"Are you kidding? After all the trouble we went to? Greg had better stare at those pictures for the next three days solid."

"So, he's..."

"Probably got them by now."

A flash of panic hit Allison's eyes. "When did you send them?"

"Right after I talked to you. I called FedEx while Dallas was in the shower."

Allison groaned and dropped into one of the kitchen chairs.

Needing more than the toasted bagel she'd had at Dallas's house, Shelby scooped two tall glasses out of the cupboard and popped the lid off the blender. "It's better this way. If I'd asked you, you would have agonized and stewed over whether or not to send the things. Now it's done. You don't have to worry about it."

"He's going to open them in the middle of a meeting. I just know he is."

Shelby grinned, handing one of the shakes to Allison. "I hope he does."

"You have an evil streak."

"No, I just have a better flair for drama than you. Imagine this, he opens them in the middle of a meeting, surrounded by lawyers and clients. He gets a glimpse of you, has to stuff them back into the envelope, force his mind back on business, and wait hours and hours and hours until he has a chance to be alone in his hotel room and take a really good look at you and the bearskin rug."

Allison stirred her shake thoughtfully. "The bearskin rug was a pretty good picture."

"I'm sure it was."

"So, you're saying, he's probably only glimpsed a breast so far."

"At the most," said Shelby. "He must be dying of anticipation."

Allison grinned. She held up her shake in a toast.

Shelby clicked her glass. "If this doesn't do the trick, you really do need to dump that man."

"Speaking of 'doing the trick,'" said Allison. "You *slept* with Dallas?"

"That I did." And parts of her were still tingling from this morning's goodbye.

Allison wiggled forward on her chair. "What was it like?"

"Not what I expected."

"Details."

"Let's just say our Dallas is not the staid, unimaginative lover we thought he was."

Allison grinned. "Well, well, well. You mean he's hot *and* he's good in bed."

Shelby made a show of fanning herself. "He's hot, and he's good in bed."

"Damn. I'm the engaged person. Why are you getting good sex?"

"I could be wrong, but I'm betting you're getting good sex on Tuesday."

The phone rang and Allison stood up. "I sure hope so."

"Wait. Don't answer that."

"Why not?"

Shelby shook her head. "It might be Greg. You don't want to talk to him. He gets nothing, *nothing* from you until Tuesday. Let the machine pick it up."

A slow smile grew on Allison's face and she sat back down. "Okay. You haven't steered me wrong so far."

"Good girl."

The machine clicked on and Allison's greeting played.

Both women stared at the telephone in anticipation.

"Allison?" It was Greg's voice all right, but he didn't sound sexy, he sounded mad. "I want to know what the hell's going on back there! I don't think this is funny. If you've got something to say to me, just spit it out. Phone me. Now."

Shelby blinked openmouthed at Allison, and Allison blinked back.

DALLAS GOT OUT of the shower to a ringing telephone. He strode quickly across the bedroom, hoping against hope it was Shelby. He'd been thinking that perhaps a one-shot deal could include an entire weekend, not just a single night.

He grabbed the receiver. "Yeah?"

"You son of a bitch!"

"Greg?"

"If I wasn't in New York, I'd be breaking down your freaking door and—"

"Whoa." Had Greg heard about Shelby? Was he this upset that Dallas had slept with their receptionist?

"Don't you whoa me."

"I had no idea you'd be this upset," said Dallas.

"No idea I'd..."

"Listen. Hey. If I'd known, I never would have done it." Now there was a lie. No force on earth could have kept him from making love with Shelby last night, nor again this morning.

"As far as I'm concerned," shouted Greg, "our partnership is dissolved right now."

"*What?*"

"Start the paperwork."

"Hey, I know I slept with her, but she was willing—"

"You *slept* with her, too?"

"What do you mean, too?"

"I mean, in addition to taking porn pictures."

Dallas's entire stomach collapsed as he clued in to Greg's mistake. "What?" was all was he able to rasp.

"They arrived in the middle of a meeting. Imagine my freaking surprise when I opened the—"

"Whoa, Greg, stop right there."

"Shut up."

"No really. No. No. You've got to listen."

The line went dead, and Dallas nearly screamed at the phone. Still dripping wet, he hung up and punched in Greg's cell number. It rang and rang, but Greg didn't pick up.

Dallas cursed out loud as he dialed directory assistance and got the hotel phone number in New York. He tapped his foot in impatience as the hotel operator put him through to Greg's room.

"Hello?"

"Shut up and listen. I mean it, Greg. I didn't take the pictures. I never saw the pictures. It was Shelby. *Shelby*. I never even opened the damned envelope!"

There was silence on the other end of the line.

"Greg? Shelby took the pictures. I *slept with Shelby*. Allison wasn't even here. She doesn't even know I *know* about the pictures." Dallas paused for a breath. "Say something, Greg."

On the other end of the phone, Greg cleared his throat. "You slept with Shelby?"

"Yeah." Dallas sat down on the bed.

"But you don't like Shelby."

"I got over it."

"Is she hot?"

"Oh, yeah. Listen, you can't let on to Allison that I know about those pictures. Shelby nearly killed herself to keep me from finding out they existed."

"You mean, she slept with you to shut you up."

"No, she didn't... Well, yeah, I guess she sort of did."

"So, my fiancée takes erotic pictures, and you get lucky?"

"Pretty much. You'll keep your mouth shut, right?"

"Uh-oh."

Dallas stilled. "What 'uh-oh'?"

"I just called Allison."

"You *what?*"

"I got her machine. Asked her what the hell was going on back there and told her to call me."

Dallas swore. "You didn't mention my name?"

"I didn't mention your name."

Dallas let out a sigh of relief, wiping one hand over his wet thigh and shaking off the water droplets. As he struggled to come up with a plan of action, the humor of the situation percolated through his brain. "You do realize that your fiancée thinks you're mad because she sent you sexy pictures."

Greg swore, and it occurred to Dallas that this was becoming a one-word conversation.

"If Shelby thought *I* was repressed, they're really going to wonder about you."

Greg swore even more colorfully. "*Fix this,*" he demanded.

It took Dallas a minute to bring his laughter under control. "Okay, we need a plan. You can't tell Allison that you talked to me, because then she'll know I know about the pictures."

"Right."

"But I can tell Shelby to pretend she talked to you and explained that the pictures weren't from me."

Greg spoke a little more hesitantly this time. "Right..."

"Don't worry, Shelby lies really well."

"Oh, good. Just what we want in a law office."

"Trust me," said Dallas. "It comes in handy."

"So, what do I do?"

Dallas smiled into the phone. "Sit back and enjoy the

photographs. Oh, and I'd show up on Tuesday with some jewelry and a really great dinner reservation if I was you. Maybe a bed-and-breakfast."

"Yeah," said Greg, his voice sounding distant.

"You're looking at them now, aren't you?"

The line went dead.

9

SHELBY BEAT DALLAS to the office on Monday morning. When he arrived, he headed straight for her desk.

"Good morning," he said, glancing at the two clients in the waiting area and at Margaret who was at the water cooler.

"Good morning," Shelby replied, trying her best to look like she hadn't banged his brains out over the weekend, and like the two of them weren't engaged in a counterespionage plot. Under the circumstances, it was a little hard to find the correct expression.

"Stop that," he hissed under his breath.

"What?"

"You look like we're plotting something."

"Sorry."

Dallas glanced over his shoulder, and Margaret gazed speculatively at them as she headed down the hall.

After Margaret left, Dallas turned back to Shelby. "Did she fall for it?"

"Allison?"

Dallas nodded.

"Yes." Shelby had made up a story about calling Greg. She told Allison that Greg was confused because the pictures had come from Dallas's apartment. Then she told Allison she'd cleared up the misunderstanding, and that Greg had sounded *very* interested in seeing Allison as soon as he got home.

"Good," said Dallas. "Coffee with Randy still on for ten?"

Shelby nodded.

"You remember what I told you?"

"Let him lead the conversation. Don't try to take over. And act naive, not Southern belle."

"I'm going to move for a continuance this afternoon. I want you to let that slip. Watch his expression when you do."

"I will."

"And come and see me when you get back."

"Roger." She had an urge to salute, but grinned instead.

Dallas grimaced. "And quit having so much fun. This isn't a game."

Shelby swallowed and sobered, almost. "Right."

Dallas sighed in disgust and turned away.

Shelby couldn't help it, she was excited at the thought of spying. Not only did she have a real job, with a real salary, in a real law firm, she was getting involved in one of their important cases.

Sure, it was only to flirt with the other team, but she swore she was going to do even better than Dallas expected. She was going to get loads of information that would help him.

Her morning crawled slowly by.

At five to ten, she gathered her purse, stopped by the ladies' room to freshen her makeup, popped a breath mint into her mouth and headed for Frappino's. Randy had beat her there, and motioned to a corner table, pointing to the coffee he'd obviously ordered for her.

She wound her way through the scattered tables and the morning crowd. "Am I late?" she asked as prettily as she could.

"I was early," he assured her. "Sit down. Sit down. I bought a few pastries." He pointed to the plate in the middle of the table. "Didn't know what you'd like."

"This is perfect," Shelby breathed. Then she smiled at him, remembering Dallas's instructions. She kept her lips firmly zipped, and let Randy start the conversation.

He pushed the pastry tray toward her. "Would you like a brownie? A croissant? A lemon tart?"

"Lemon," she said, reaching out. It looked like the sexiest thing to eat. No harm in reducing Randy's brain power. She set the tart on a napkin beside her coffee.

"All set for another week?" asked Randy.

"Yes, I am." She dipped her index finger into the lemon filling, then licked it clean. "Mmm. Great choice."

Randy cleared his throat. "Anything exciting going on this week?"

Shelby made a show of pondering hard. "Not that I can think of off hand."

"I saw something in the newspaper about Perth... I think it was Perth-Abercrombie and embezzlement?"

Shelby nodded, but didn't offer any information. Make him dig a little harder.

"Isn't that Dallas Williams's case?"

She snapped her fingers. "You know, you're right. It is. As a matter of fact, Dallas was talking to Allan about it just this morning..."

Randy leaned forward, the interest level in his eyes leaping. "And..."

She broke off a section of the tart and placed it on her tongue. "Something about the courthouse."

"Yes. The hearing starts this afternoon," Randy prompted.

"He's asking for a...continuation..."

Randy's eyes got wider. "Continuance?"

"That's it."

"Why?"

Shelby shrugged and took another bit of the tart. "I dunno."

"Did they say anything else?" He cleared his throat and backed off. "I mean, I find that very interesting."

"Really? I find it pretty boring. Brokerage houses. I mean, what's the big deal?"

Randy smiled a little condescendingly. "They're a very big deal. They help rich people invest in the stock market, buy bonds, move money."

No kidding, Einstein. Shelby blinked, trying to look impressed.

"Why don't you ask Dallas some more about the case? I bet you'd find his take on it more interesting than what's in the newspaper."

"Ask him what?"

Randy shrugged again, stirring his coffee before taking a drink. "Maybe his approach to the prosecution. The evidence. What financial records they plan to use."

"I don't know..."

"Go for it," said Randy. "Maybe we could meet again tomorrow and talk?" His gaze softened on her face. "I find you a very beautiful and very fascinating woman."

Shelby pretended to be flattered. "I'd like that."

Randy stood up and took her hand, helping her to rise. "Let me walk you to the lobby."

She resisted the urge to pull her hand out of his grasp. She was determined to impress Dallas. And letting Randy think she was attracted to him seemed like the best method at the moment.

When they stopped in front of the elevators, he turned to face her—too close, way too close.

"Tomorrow?" he whispered.

"Tomorrow," she agreed, trying to look like his slick, salesman come-on had appealed to her.

She must have hit the right note, because he leaned forward unexpectedly and kissed her.

Damn. This was not what she wanted. But she stayed still, even let her lips soften. But when his tongue flicked out, she quickly backed off.

She stepped away. "Thanks for the coffee."

His lips curved into a self-satisfied smile. "My pleasure."

Shelby quickly turned away before her shudder could show on her face. She made her way back upstairs, wishing she had a toothbrush. But a quick trip to the ladies' room to rinse her mouth and pop another breath mint was the best she could do.

Then she headed down the office hallway. Margaret saw her and closely watched her progress.

Shelby gave her an open, innocent smile and knocked on Dallas's door.

"Come in," he called.

She slipped inside and closed the door behind her.

Dallas stood up from his chair, a frown on his face. "Playing both sides against the middle, are we?"

Shelby stopped, glancing quickly behind her to see if he was talking to someone else. The office was empty. She turned back to Dallas. "Huh?"

"Tell me." He strolled around the end of the desk, tossing a pen onto the desktop. "What's your real relationship to Randy?"

Shelby squinted.

"What did you do?" asked Dallas. "Go down there and tell him every damn thing I said?"

It occurred to Shelby that she may have been too quick to trust Dallas. Maybe he was actually a psycho.

"Well?" he asked, moving toward her.

She debated screaming and running from the room, but then decided there wasn't much he could do to her in the middle of an office full of people. She folded her arms over her chest. "I have absolutely no idea what you're talking about."

His smile turned menacing. "I saw the kiss."

"The kiss?"

"I saw you kiss Randy."

"I didn't kiss Randy."

Dallas leaned forward, glaring at her.

"Oh, good grief." She threw up her hands. "*That* wasn't a kiss." Then she squared her shoulders and stepped up in front of him.

This served him bloody well right.

She took his cheeks between her palms and pulled him in for a hot, openmouthed, long-lasting kiss that came from her soul.

"*That*." She backed off. "Was a kiss. I was playacting with Randy."

Dallas blinked in silence, lips parted, expression looking as if it had frozen in place.

"You told me I was supposed to get information from him." She paused. "Dallas?" She snapped her fingers in front of his face.

"You're incorrigible," he growled.

"Yeah? Well, you'll have to spank me later."

"*Excuse* me?"

Shelby grinned. "You are such an easy target."

"You think I wouldn't spank you?"

Shelby rocked her head back and forth, grinning in delight. "My, my, Dallas. For a staid guy, you definitely have a kinky side."

He leaned in, wrapping one arm around her waist and hauling her flush against his torso. "I can have any side you want me to have."

"I won't have an affair with you."

"I don't want an affair. I just want sex."

"Sex once, is just sex. Even twice. But once you hit three times, it's an affair."

"We already had sex three times."

"We counted the first two as one, remember?"

"I like that logic. So can three and four count as one, so we'd only be at two?"

Shelby grinned. "Afraid not. Too much time has passed."

"Your eyes are jade again."

"What?"

"Never mind. Just a personal cross to bear. So, that's it? We're done forever?"

"Once more, and it's an affair. And, let's face it, Dallas. We liked it. We'd probably keep going. And if we hit ten, we're in a relationship. Then I'm back to dating my boss, and you have to start taking me to parties where I'll embarrass you, and you'll lose all your clients."

Dallas took a deep breath. "Which means I have to let go of you now."

"If you don't want to ruin both of our lives, yes."

Dallas swore. "What about kissing?"

"Kissing leads to sex." She dropped her gaze to his full lips, trying hard not to think about what she was giving up. "Especially with you."

"You're killin' me here, Shelby."

"I got some information from Randy."

His eyebrows jumped. "Well, if I can't take you on the desktop, I suppose I'll have to settle for that."

"Good choice." Shelby pulled back while she still could. "He wants me to talk to you about the case."

Dallas retreated around his desk once again, motioning for her to take one of the guest chairs. "Go on."

"He said I should ask you about your approach to the prosecution, the evidence and what financial records you plan to use."

Dallas rocked back, the playfulness completely leaving his face. This was the Dallas she'd first met—the one she wanted on her side. The one she didn't want going up against her.

"They *already* know which financial records we plan to use," he said. "The ones that show their client, Ralph McQueen, siphoned off three-hundred-thousand dollars. Which means..."

His jaw tightened and he hit the intercom button on his desk. "Margaret?"

"Yes?"

"Can you have someone bring in the evidence boxes for the Perth-Abercrombie case?"

There was a pause at Margaret's end. "All of them?"

"All of them."

Shelby sat up straight. "Oh, good. Now she'll know we're not having an affair."

"What?"

"Margaret's not stupid. I bet your last receptionist didn't have lengthy meetings in here with the door closed."

Dallas's eye narrowed.

Oops. Not a good time for a joke.

The door opened and the mailroom boy came in balancing two cardboard boxes, one of top of the other.

Shelby jumped up and moved her chair out of the way.

"Put them on the floor in the corner," said Dallas.

"There are twenty more," said the boy.

"Bring 'em all," said Dallas.

"Can I help?" asked Shelby.

Dallas clasped the back of his neck with his hand. "It would sure be a lot easier if we knew what we were looking for."

"I did a lot of work with the financial records at Terra Suma."

He shot her a look of disbelief. "That was a cocktail lounge, not a brokerage house."

Shelby tried to hide her disappointment. "Right. Okay." She moved toward the door. Maybe flirting was more her area of expertise.

"Wait," said Dallas.

She stopped.

"I have to go to the courthouse now, and it'll take a few days to get the accounting team reassembled." He lifted box number one and put it on his conference table. "What we know is that McQueen siphoned off money about a half penny at a time."

Shelby moved toward the open box. "Half a penny?"

"He rounded up on transaction commissions. Millions and millions of transaction commissions. Never enough that any individual client would notice. And if anyone did come across an individual transaction, they'd call it a rounding error and wouldn't care. But, systemically, over two years, he amassed a whole lot of money."

"And they fired him."

"They fired him, and are suing for damages." He paused. "Now that you mention it, if you've got time, I could use somebody to go through these and recheck McQueen's commissions. Maybe there's something we missed." He pulled out a stack of papers. "The ones highlighted in yellow are his." He gazed down at Shelby. "You game?"

Shelby couldn't help a surge of excitement at the thought of doing real investigative work, and a quieter surge of pride that he trusted her. "Sure."

OVER THE COURSE of twenty-four hours, Dallas watched his orderly law office turn to pandemonium. Shelby had discovered there were additional evidence boxes in the storage locker that the accountants had deemed irrelevant, and a delivery service was bringing in every scrap of information for five city blocks. They'd hired a temporary receptionist to free up Shelby's time, and she was right in the thick of things, directing operations between the reception area, the photocopy room and Dallas's office.

Adding to the turmoil, Greg had called in saying he'd be a couple of days late getting back to the office—Dallas didn't have to be a rocket scientist to figure out what that was about. Not that he blamed Greg. Quite frankly, he'd like nothing better than to spirit Shelby away for a few days at a hidden hotel.

While he watched her from the shadow of his office door, Allan appeared in the hall beside him.

"I told you so," said Allan.

"You told me what?" asked Dallas, fighting a shot of guilt for watching Shelby when he should have been working. It wasn't like he hadn't been here at six o'clock this morning.

"I told you to give her a chance." Allan nodded to where Shelby was talking to a deliveryman. There was a definite trace of laughter in his voice. "Once you get over her legs, she's pretty good."

Uh-uh. Dallas wasn't getting drawn into that conversation. He definitely wasn't over her legs, or any other part of her anatomy, yet. "Greg leave you a phone number where we can reach him?"

Allan smirked at Dallas's obvious change of topic. Just then another man came through the office door. This one glanced around and headed straight for Shelby. He didn't exactly look like a deliveryman, and he was too purposeful to be a new client...

"I tried Greg's cell, but it must be turned off," said Dallas, watching the man with growing suspicion. What was he all about?

"Greg's on vacation," said Allan. "He deserves a rest from this place."

"We all do."

"Shelby Jacobs?" The strange man's voice carried across the reception area.

"Yes," Shelby answered with a nod.

The man reached into his inside breast pocket.

"Summons," muttered Allan at the same time the realization hit Dallas.

Dallas bolted across the room.

The man handed her an envelope. "You've been served." He turned to walk away, leaving Shelby blinking in surprise.

"Let me see it," Dallas demanded, wondering what he'd missed about Shelby's relevance to McQueen's case.

Shelby pulled the envelope protectively toward her chest. "It's for me."

"I'm your lawyer."

She slipped her fingertip under the flap and worked open the envelope. "For about fifteen minutes." She pulled out the folded paper. "A week and a half ago." She opened up the summons. "And I never paid you, so I don't think it counts."

Dallas tried to read over her shoulder, but she turned so he couldn't see.

"You'd better tell me *everything* you know about Calloway and McQueen," he demanded. "No holding back this time, we need to know what we're up against." No matter what, Dallas didn't want her incriminating herself on the stand.

She shot him a look of disbelief. "It's not *your* trial I've been summoned to."

"It's not?"

"Jeez, Dallas. You have such a suspicious mind."

No, he didn't. Well, not particularly.

He was just experienced. Experienced enough to be...well...suspicious.

Okay. He'd give her that one. "Who else would send you a summons?"

"It's for Gerry's trial tomorrow."

"Gerry?"

"You remember. Gerry Bonnaducci. My old boss. They don't give you much notice, do they?"

"Gerry's the gunrunner from the Game-O-Rama?"

"Right."

Now Dallas was even more worried. Talk about the potential to incriminate herself.

He reached for the summons again. "I'll represent you."

She pulled it away, arching her eyebrows. "At your prices, forget it."

"I'm not going to *charge you.*" What kind of a man did she think he was?

She refolded the summons, stuffing it back into the envelope. "I'm a witness, Dallas, not a suspect. And you have too much work already." She waved him away. "I'll just take a coffee break and pop down there—"

"But if they get you up on the stand—"

"What?" Now she looked annoyed. "I'll break down and confess to buying Uzi's from the Russian mafia?"

"They might get you to say something—"

"I didn't *do* anything, Dallas. They're not going to get me to say that I did." Her tone turned wry. "But thanks for the vote of confidence."

"You need professional—"

"I believe she said no." It was Allan's deep, disapproving voice from behind him.

"Thank you, Allan," said Shelby. Then, with a triumphant glare at Dallas, she tipped her nose slightly upward and headed for the photocopy room where they were stacking dusty boxes of Perth-Abercrombie evidence files. She dropped the summons into her desk drawer on the way past.

"She can't go in there cold," Dallas protested, itching to get his hands on that summons. He didn't even have the most rudimentary details of the case. He should have looked into it further when he'd sprung her from the Haines Street lockup last week.

"You actually think she's guilty?" asked Allan.

"Of course not." Not really. Well, not of buying Uzi's from the Russian mafia.

"They have a name for lawyers who force their services on people," Allan pointed out.

"That Gerry Bonnaducci struck me as a scumbag. I wouldn't put it past him to set her up to take his fall. Who knows how the guy's connected, or who they've hired, or what they'll try to do to her?"

Allan grinned. "Not that you're feeling overprotective or anything."

"I'm looking at this as a lawyer."

"You're looking at this as a lover."

Dallas stilled. "A *what?*"

Allan grinned smugly.

"What did Greg tell you?"

"I haven't talked to Greg since he left for New York. But Margaret's got her theories."

"That's exactly what Margaret's got," Dallas scoffed, relaxing a little. "Theories, and nothing else."

He and Shelby weren't lovers. They weren't even having a fling. And he wasn't getting overprotective, he was merely trying to give the woman the benefit of his professional advice. She was his employee, for God's sake. And, innocent or guilty, everyone needed a lawyer if they were going to court.

He couldn't in good conscience let her end up in jail because she was stubborn and pigheaded. He glanced into the photocopy room. Seeing she was busy, and working with her back to the door, he headed for her desk.

"Dallas?" Allan's voice was a warning. "What are you—"

"You should probably leave the room," said Dallas, sliding open her desk drawer.

"That's illegal," said Allan.

"I'm looking for a paperclip."

"Don't make me fire you."

"You can't fire me, I'm your partner."

"I can report you to the law society."

"Report me for getting a paperclip and, oops, picking a letter up off the floor?"

Allan's footsteps sounded on the carpet. "Don't you open—"

"It fell out."

"*What* are you doing?" Shelby's voice this time.

"He's snooping into your private mail," said Allan. "You want to press charges?"

Dallas straightened, unfolding the summons. "Of course she doesn't want to press charges. We have an understanding, don't we, Shelby? You get free rein of my briefcase, and I get free rein of your drawers."

There was a moment's silence after his last word. Shelby might have been annoyed with him, but she was still forced to bite down on a smirk.

A split second later Allan's face broke out in a grin. "If he's been messing around in your drawers, you've got an even bigger lawsuit than I thought."

"I'll take the fifth on what Dallas has been doing in my drawers," said Shelby.

"I could represent you," Allan offered.

"How much do you think I'd get?"

Dallas ignored them both, noting the time and place on the summons. "I'm just going to make a few discrete inquiries, so that you'll know what you're up against."

Allan turned a laugh into a cough. "Whether she was up against the wall, up against the desk, or up against the bookcase, it all translates into thousands of dollars in damages." He shifted his gaze to Shelby. "Dallas pays. You get a settlement. I get the fees. It's all good."

Shelby eyed Dallas with suspicion. "Did you *tell* him about us?"

"No, I didn't tell him. But *you* just did." The woman was never going to survive on the witness stand.

Allan leaned toward Shelby, dropping his voice to a faux conspiratorial tone. "I could tell he had the hots for you the minute he started talking about your legs."

"He likes my legs?"

"Oh, he's—"

"Will you two *stop?*" Dallas demanded. "This is no time for jokes."

Shelby whisked the summons from his hand. "You're the one who needs to stop. I'm an intelligent woman who didn't break any laws. I'll drop down to the courthouse tomorrow, tell the truth, and come on back to work. I wish you'd have a little faith in me."

10

LOOKED LIKE SHELBY'S wish was destined to go unfulfilled. As she took her seat in the witness stand, and swore to tell the truth, the whole truth, she spotted Dallas lurking in the back of the courtroom. He slid into an aisle seat next to the door guard.

He was obviously afraid she'd screw up and end up in handcuffs. How flattering.

She caught his gaze and glared her displeasure at him.

He stared right back, looking determined and implacable, kind of like a pet pit bull ready to growl at the ice-cream man. For a split second, she found it endearing. Then she found it annoying. But then she found it endearing again.

"Miss Jacobs," began Eugene Shuster, the defense attorney for Gerry Bonnaducci.

Shelby shifted her attention to the short, balding, slicked-over haired, tight-suited Mr. Shuster. Dallas and the rest of the sparse audience became fuzzy shapes in her soft vision.

"Please tell the court how long you've lived in Chicago."

How long she'd lived in Chicago?

Oh, yeah. She could see now that these were very dangerous questions. Good thing her pit bull had showed up. Maybe she could make a leash and leather collar joke later...

She couldn't help sliding him a knowing glance.

His eyes narrowed in annoyance.

"Miss Jacobs?" prompted the lawyer.

Shelby quickly returned her attention to Shuster. "Four weeks," she answered.

"And where did you live before moving to Chicago?"

Another one that ought to get her ten years in the slammer. "Minneapolis."

"And what did you do in Minneapolis?"

"I was a cocktail waitress."

"Where?"

Shelby sat back, cocking head to one side, trying to figure out why they were wasting time on mundane details. "The Terra Suma Cocktail Lounge."

"What was the name of the owner of the Terra Suma Cocktail Lounge?"

"Neil Hessel."

"And how would you characterize your relationship with Mr. Hessel?"

Okay, now *that* she hadn't expected. This guy had obviously asked around about her. "He was my boss and my boyfriend."

Shuster got a sly, almost voyeuristic gleam in his eyes. "So, you were having sex with your boss?"

Shelby felt her shoulders tense. Talk about irrelevant. But there was no way in the world she was letting Mr. Oily Comb-Over embarrass her. "Yes. Generally once a week. He preferred the missionary position, but sometimes—"

The judge's gavel came down on the bench. "Just answer the question," he said.

Shelby snapped her mouth shut. She caught Dallas's look of stupefaction and presumed it was because of her irreverence rather than the fact her ex-boyfriend preferred the missionary position.

Well, hell, what kind of a question *was* that? Shuster deserved the answer he got.

Shuster cleared his throat. "Miss Jacobs. Were you aware that your boss and lover gambled?"

"Yes."

Dallas suddenly dropped his chin to his chest in a posture of defeat.

What? What was wrong with that answer?

He was throwing her off here. She forced herself to pull her attention away from Dallas, absently taking in the other members of the audience—a casually dressed man in his mid-thirties taking notes on a small pad, a woman knitting something pink, her needles clicking away, two spruced-up but worn-looking men who were probably next on the docket—

"What did he bet on?" Shuster took a step toward her, shrugging his shoulders, assuming an air of nonchalance. "Horses, baseball, poker?"

Shelby nodded. "Yes."

"Did you know the name of his bookie?"

Bookie? That question confused Shelby. "What do you mean?"

"Yes or no. Did you know the name of your boss's bookie?"

Shelby gave in to temptation and glanced at Dallas again. He made a frantic hand motion in front of his chest. He looked like an umpire calling a player safe, which really didn't give her clue one about how to answer.

"No," she answered slowly, trying to figure out what the heck Dallas was signaling back there.

"Did it bother you that he gambled?" asked Shuster.

"I thought it was a waste of money," said Shelby. "But it was his money."

"Did you ever help him?"

She could see Dallas's jaw getting tighter and his eyes narrowing as the muscles in his face tensed up.

"Help him how?" she asked.

"Drive him to the track, go to the bank for him, take a phone call..."

Of course she'd done those things. What girlfriend didn't?

"Yes or no?" prompted Shuster.

"Yes," said Shelby.

Dallas stood up and moved down the aisle, past the knitting woman, past the man taking notes. As he sat down in the front row behind the prosecuting attorney, he made a slashing motion across his neck.

What? She was supposed to stop answering? She'd sworn to tell the whole truth.

"So, you didn't mind that your boss was breaking the law," said Shuster.

"Breaking the—"

"Yes or no? You said you went to the bank for him, took phone calls in connection with his gambling habit—presumably from his bookie—drove him to the track, who knows what all else. Did you encourage him to break the law?"

Shelby glanced at Dallas.

He shook his head.

"No," said Shelby firmly.

"Did you report his crimes to the police?"

"I never knew—"

"Yes or no, Miss Jacobs. Your employer was breaking the law. You've admitted you knew he was breaking the law, yet you never reported it to the police. You were encouraging him, at the very least, enabling him. Did you profit from his crimes?"

Shelby looked to Dallas.

He shook his head, but she couldn't tell if that was the answer or if he was frustrated with her.

"No," said Shelby.

"Come on, Miss Jacobs. You expect us to believe you didn't profit from his crimes?"

Shelby looked at the judge. "Do I have to keep answering these questions?"

The judge looked surprised. "Yes. You *are* under oath."

"But he's making it sound—"

"Let's explore a scenario," said Shuster, strolling across in front of the judge's bench, then turning to stroll back. "You knew your boss was engaged in illegal gambling. But since you profited from it—clothes, expensive jewelry, trips…"

"I never—"

"You not only turned a blind eye, you actually helped him commit those crimes for personal gain."

"I thought he only bet on racehorses." She saw Dallas lean forward and hand a note to the prosecuting attorney.

Shuster chuckled dryly. "Come on, Miss Jacobs, you expect us to believe—"

The prosecuting attorney jumped to his feet. "Your Honor, Miss Jacobs is not on trial here."

Shuster spun to stare at the man. Then he turned his attention to the judge. "I'm establishing a pattern of behavior."

"Your Honor," said the prosecuting attorney. "If this line of questioning is to continue, I think Miss Jacobs has the right to speak to her attorney."

"Are *you* her attorney?" asked the judge.

"No. But her attorney is in the court."

The judge turned to Shelby. "Do you wish to speak to your attorney?"

"I wish to tell the *truth*," said Shelby.

Dallas came partway out of his seat.

"Very well," said the judge. "Tell the truth."

Dallas sat back down, and Shelby refused to meet his eyes. Instead, she glared pointedly at Shuster. "Can I speak without him interrupting me?"

"You may," said the judge.

"Good." Shelby squared her shoulders. Her gaze rested on Gerry at the defense table for a moment. You'd think the man would be embarrassed at trying to blame her for his crimes. But he stared impassively back. She guessed all was fair in larceny and theft.

"I didn't know my former boss was engaged in anything illegal," she began, taking in the entire courtroom as she spoke.

"Yes, I knew he gambled, but I only knew he bet on horse races, which is perfectly legal. I never called his bookie, and I don't know his bookie's name, because I didn't know he *had* a bookie. Yes, I slept with him. We were both consenting adults at the time, and we certainly didn't engage in anything illegal in the bedroom. In fact, our sex life was pretty boring."

Shelby took a breath. "I'm not some partner in crime who's helping her bosses pull off felonies. Apparently, they're doing that all by themselves.

"I buy my designer clothes at warehouse outlets, my jewelry is cubic zirconia, and I'm currently living with a friend while I try to get on my feet financially. If Neil broke the law, I didn't know about it. If Gerry broke the law, I didn't know about it. I worked at Game-O-Rama for less than a week, selling game tokens and cleaning up spilled popcorn. Believe me, nobody was more surprised than me to get arrested for it—"

"Your *Honor*," Shuster protested.

Shelby glanced at the judge in time to see him cover a smirk.

Then he quickly cleared his expression. "Any further questions, Mr. Shuster?"

Shuster hesitated for a moment. "Nothing further," he mumbled.

"Mr. Simpson?" The judge addressed the prosecuting attorney.

He stood up. "I think she's about covered it."

The judge turned to Shelby. "The witness may step down."

Shelby breathed a chopped sigh of satisfaction, and stepped out of the witness stand. She presumed she was free to leave the courtroom, so she headed between the attorney's tables and opened the mini gate.

Dallas fell into step beside her, muttering under his breath. "You've got horseshoes stuffed firmly—"

"I'll have you know that was skill not luck," she muttered back.

Dallas pushed open the courtroom door. "Ha. I'll have *you* know he was leading you down the garden path."

They passed into the foyer, where the clicking of a dozen heels echoed against the high ceiling, and a stained glass mural at one end of the corridor made a dappled pattern on the polished floor.

"And I recognized the garden path," she pointed out. "And got myself out of there."

Dallas pushed open the heavy main door and they crossed onto the wide concrete steps. Heel clicks were replaced by horn honks and the sounds of engines revving along Barkley Street.

"If the judge hadn't been sympathetic, Shuster would have backed you into a corner you couldn't escape from. I want you to promise me you will *never* do that again without letting me talk you through your testimony. What the hell was Simpson thinking, bringing you in cold?"

Shelby started down the wide, semicircular staircase. "You know Mr. Simpson?"

"No. And I don't particularly want to, either."

"He *did* object on your behalf."

"He should have thought of it himself. I practically had to light a fire under his butt."

"That would have been entertaining."

Dallas took a right when they came to the sidewalk. "Remember, only fifty percent of lawyers graduated in the top half of their class."

Shelby followed his lead, presuming he'd brought his car. "Did you?"

"You bet."

She shifted a little closer to his side as the crowd

thickened. "You know, you're kind of sweet when you get all protective."

"I'm not protective and I'm *not* sweet. I'm pissed. I'm pissed at you, and I'm pissed at Simpson. That could have been a complete and total disaster."

"But it wasn't."

Dallas took a deep breath. "No, it wasn't."

"The truth won out."

Dallas stopped dead in the middle of the sidewalk, turning to face her with a grave expression, forcing the stream of pedestrians to part and go around them. "A smart lawyer in the audience won out."

She couldn't help the grin that crept over her face. "You're so humble."

"I'm not trying to massage my ego, I'm trying to warn you about messing around with the law without proper advice."

"Forgive me if my memory is failing, but it seems to me *I* did all the talking."

"Yeah? Well, *I* gave you the opening. And you wouldn't have had to do all that talking if we'd planned your testimony in advance."

Shelby threw up her hands. "Fine. You're brilliant and I'm hopeless."

The corner of Dallas's mouth twitched. "At least we've got that straight."

He turned and they started walking again.

"You have to admit," she said, "once I got rolling, I was pretty good."

Dallas didn't answer, and when she glanced up, he had a distracted look in his eyes. "So, was your sex life with Neil really boring?"

"I swore on a bible to tell the truth up there."

"You ever going to say that about me on a witness stand?"

Shelby let him wait for a minute before she drawled out her answer. "I think under those circumstances, I'd have to take the fifth."

"Ouch."

"Teach you to fish for compliments."

DALLAS WANTED TO FISH for a whole lot more than compliments from Shelby.

For the third day in a row, she sat cross-legged on his office floor, surrounded by piles of papers and open boxes of Perth-Abercrombie evidence. She was wearing teal-blue leather pants and a matching cropped jacket decorated with silver rivets. From his angle, standing up, it was obvious she wore nothing but a lace bra beneath. And, yes, her navel *was* showing.

Dallas sucked in a breath as he picked up a file from his desktop, trying to tamp down the buzz of sexual desire that had become his constant companion. It was impossible to get used to working with a goddess—especially one that crawled around on his floor and flashed her bright smile every thirty seconds or so.

Like now.

She tipped her head and grinned up at him. "How was the meeting?"

"Eamon is anxious to get to the hearing and get this over with. The publicity is hurting business. You know, if he ever walks in here, I'm going to have one hell of a time explaining what you're doing."

"Think he remembers me from the party?"

"Oh, he remembers you all right." In fact, Eamon had

offered to introduce Dallas to a few eligible women from his own social circle—instead of his daughter's.

Dallas's phone rang, and he reached across the desk to pick it up.

"Hello?"

"Dallas? It's Allison. Is Shelby handy?"

Dallas closed his eyes for a split second, then he held the receiver out to Shelby. "It's for you."

She jumped to her feet, not looking the least bit surprised to be receiving calls on his line.

He held his hand over the mouthpiece. "Next time you fix my partner's love life, can you do something that won't keep him away from the office indefinitely?"

"He's only been back in Chicago for three days," said Shelby. "Three days isn't too much to ask for a happily-ever-after."

Dallas snorted his disgust. It had been closer to four days. It was ten o'clock Friday morning, and there was no sign of Greg. He sure hoped Greg and Allison were having a whole lot of fun at the Starview Bed-and-Breakfast, because he was working his butt off back here, staring at Shelby for *far* too many hours each day.

Shelby took the receiver from his hand. "Hello?"

She grinned broadly, her eyes sparking with lime-green delight. "Things still going good up there?"

She paused. "You mean, he's run out of steam already?"

A wider grin. "Oh. Okay then."

"You are?"

"Really?"

She stared up at Dallas, looking like she had just won the lottery. "That's fantastic news!"

"Is Greg coming back?" asked Dallas hopefully.

Shelby put her hand on his chest.

He wasn't sure whether that was to shut him up, or just to torture him. Either way, he was enough of a masochist to shut up, stay still, and leave her hand just where it was.

"Absolutely," said Shelby, unconsciously rubbing his chest. "I'd love to help."

Dallas resisted the urge to wrap his hand around hers.

"Great," said Shelby. "See you tonight. Bye."

She leaned across Dallas to hang up the phone, dropping her hand.

He remembered to breathe.

"They're getting married," she squealed.

"We already knew that," Dallas pointed out. "Is Greg coming to the office today?"

"Next weekend."

"He's not coming in until next weekend?"

Shelby rolled her eyes. "They're getting married next weekend. Friday night. They've set a date, and they're getting married in seven days."

He was losing Greg again in seven days? "They're not planning a long honeymoon, are they?"

Shelby pushed against Dallas's chest. This time he did capture her hand.

"Don't be such a bear."

He hung on tight. "I'm the one looking after his caseload."

"Well, Allison says they're coming home today. I'm sure he'll be in the office next week."

Thank goodness for that. The Perth-Abercrombie hearing was set for next Friday morning, and Dallas needed to be able to focus on it.

"I'm going to help Allison find a dress," said Shelby, nearly dancing with delight. "And I'm going to be the maid of honor. The wedding will be small, just fifty or so." She paused for a breath and stared up into Dallas's eyes. "I can't believe how well those pictures worked."

The memory of the pictures brought back a memory of Shelby's striptease, which brought back memories of making love, which reminded him that he was slowly going insane.

"Shelby?"

"Yeah?"

"You *sure* we can't have an affair?"

She glanced away. It might have been his imagination, but her voice sounded overbright. "Who's got time for an affair? I've got a wedding to plan."

"You want to help me plan the bachelor party?" Dallas figured she'd do a way better job.

"You're the best man?"

He nodded.

She laughed. "Well, if we can't make love, at least we get to dance at the wedding."

He shifted a little closer. "I have a feeling it won't be quite the same."

"Dallas," she sighed.

"I want you."

"We can't."

"Right now."

"Oh, sure. We'll just lock the door and get it on on your desk."

"We could," he pointed out, feeling just insane enough to do it.

"Get real."

"What about tonight?"

"I'm going wedding dress shopping tonight."

"Stores close at nine."

She stared at him with genuine regret. "I wish I could, Dallas. Really I do."

He leaned in. "You can."

"I have to be strong."

"No, you don't."

She grinned. "And you call *me* incorrigible."

"Oh, yeah. Seems to me I owe you a spanking. Turn around and bend over."

"If your clients could hear you now, they'd have a heart attack."

"And drop your pants."

"Yeah. Like that's gonna happen."

Dallas grinned. "And you call *me* staid and conservative."

"Not anymore."

He grunted. "At least that's progress."

She slipped her hand from beneath his and pointed to her watch. "You're late for your meeting."

He knew that. But, God help him, he didn't want to leave. And not just because he wanted to make love. Because he wanted to tease her, challenge her, and have her challenge him right back. In fact, he probably would have been disappointed if she'd caved right away.

Okay, so that was a lie. He'd have loved it if she'd caved.

She circled behind him and pushed against his back. "Go. Before Margaret makes any more assumptions about us."

"Wish Margaret was right," he muttered.

"Have a nice meeting."

"Greg gets to have all the fun."

11

"You look stunning," said Shelby as Allison pirouetted on the small dais in front of a mirrored wall in the bridal shop. The dress was champagne in color, with a strapless, cotton-eyelet bodice, and a full, calf-length skirt of silk organza. A wide satin ribbon emphasized her waist, and she practically floated when she walked.

"At least it doesn't have a twenty-foot train," said Allison.

Shelby walked around the side to look from a different angle. Allison didn't want to go too formal, and the dresses they'd looked at last night were all over the top.

"If we put your hair up," said Shelby, "and weave in a few flowers, it'll be perfect. It's bridal, yet not fru-fru or fairy princess."

"What do you want to wear?" asked Allison.

"We have a matching bridesmaid dress," said the attendant. "Dusty-rose, or jewel-blue. The skirt's not as full, and the bodice matches."

"Is this the one?" Shelby asked Allison.

Allison grinned. "I think so."

"Dusty-rose," said Shelby. "I don't want to outshine the bride."

The attendant headed across the shop to a long rack of colored dresses, while Shelby and Allison grinned stupidly at each other.

"I'm getting married," Allison whispered.

"You sure are," said Shelby.

"It was fantastic," said Allison.

"Greg or the B and B?"

"Greg, the B and B, *everything*."

"As your maid of honor, I feel duty-bound to say 'I told you so.'"

"You sure did," said Allison. "And you went *way* above and beyond the call of duty. Think I'd better pay for your dress."

"Oh, no, you don't."

"Okay. We'll let Greg pay for it."

Shelby grinned. "Deal."

"Speaking of above and beyond... You go *above and beyond* with Dallas while I was away?"

"He's my *boss*." Not to say she hadn't been tempted. More tempted than she'd ever thought possible. It was embarrassing, but even his "turn around and bend over" line had turned her on. Which was pathetic, since she wasn't a turn-around-and-bend-over kind of girl.

"I take it that's a no?"

"Yes, it's a no. I've sworn off bosses, remember?"

"You made one exception."

"That was in the line of duty."

"But you wanted to do it again, right?"

Shelby hesitated, not sure if confessing to Allison would make things worse or better. Right now she was a walking case of hormones. She was Eve, and Dallas was the forbidden fruit.

"You're blushing," Allison laughed. "That is *so* definitely a yes."

"Shouldn't we be talking about you?" asked Shelby. "This is *your* wedding."

Allison waved a dismissive hand. "We figured my relationship out last week. Now it's your turn."

"It's hardly the same thing."

Allison twisted one way, and then the other, letting the gorgeous full skirt swirl around her legs. "You know, vowing never to sleep with your boss is like vowing never to sleep with red-headed men."

"Red-headed men can't fire me."

"Dallas isn't going to fire you. What I mean is, each case should be taken on its merits."

"You mean, how great it would be to get laid, versus how awful it would be to get fired."

"Exactly." Allison grinned and waggled her eyebrows. "You can always get another job."

The attendant returned with the dusty-rose bridesmaid dress draped over one arm. "It's a size four," she said. "Sound about right?"

Shelby took the dress. "Sounds right. Thanks."

"I'll wait here," said Allison, still gazing at herself in the huge mirror. The distracted glow in her eyes said the dress was right.

Shelby ducked into the changing room and slipped out of her clothes.

In her opinion, it would feel pretty darned crappy to get fired. Especially from her first real job. Especially when she'd just been given some extra responsibility on the Perth-Abercrombie case.

For the first time in her life, she felt like she had a professional future. And Dallas was a great boss, as long as she ignored her sexual yearnings.

Of course, everything would go to hell if they had a fling and broke up. Then there'd be tension, probably animosity. Even if he was comfortable working with an ex, she knew she'd never be.

She pulled the bridesmaid dress over her head, and reached back to do up the zipper. The fit was good. The dress was pretty, but it was understated enough to keep her in the background. Which was exactly what she wanted.

She opened the change room door.

"What do you think?" She moved next to Allison in front of the mirror so they could see the effect of the dresses side by side.

"Style suits me a bit better, I think," said Allison.

"That's what we want," said Shelby. "If we play up your jewelry and hair, and play mine down—"

Allison frowned. "I want you to look pretty."

Shelby spread her arms. "Hey, I'm not exactly a dog in this."

"You wouldn't be a dog in anything."

Shelby bumped her shoulder against Allison's. "It's your day to shine. And I like this dress. It's a bit conservative, but nothing I'd pick would work in a wedding anyway. Besides, Dallas will probably like it."

"You going to sleep with him after the reception?"

The attendant suddenly took a few discreet steps back, taking an intense interest in a veil hanging on the wall.

"Of course not," said Shelby.

"I think we should get you some killer underwear in case you change your mind. You know, conservative to siren with one little zipper."

Shelby chuckled. "I'm not going to change my mind. I am strong."

"You are misguided."

"I want a job more than I want sex."

Maybe. Hopefully. Please, oh, please, let her want the job more than she wanted sex.

"It *is* possible to have both, you know," Allison pointed out.

"Not in this case." Shelby turned to get a side view of the dress. "So, we're gonna take these?"

"You sure about yours?"

"I'm positive."

Allison grinned. "Let's buy them."

HAVING DECIDED that their own tuxes would work just fine for the wedding, Dallas and Greg were an hour early for their dinner with Shelby and Allison. To save time, the bride and groom had decided on a celebratory dinner with best man and maid of honor instead of a shower and a bachelor party.

Dallas had brought both gag sex gifts and kitchenware. He never would have thought of gifts at all, if Shelby hadn't phoned him this morning with a list, saying she was too busy, and could he please sign both their names. He didn't normally shop for women, but he'd somehow gotten into the habit of saying yes to anything Shelby wanted.

Though he had to admit, the gifts were a good idea. Even though it was rushed, he wanted Allison and Greg to have a fantastic wedding.

The men took a seat at the bar in The Library—the restaurant's lounge. The room was heavily accented in wood. The lights were dim, with a yellow cast. Tufted armchairs and overstuffed couches surrounded low, maple-and-glass tables. The walls were decorated with bookshelves, following up on the theme of the name, and the windows were covered in wooden shutters.

"So, you haven't figured out what Calloway is fishing for?" asked Greg after they'd each ordered a single malt.

Dallas shook his head. "Shelby fed him some more information yesterday. Nothing he doesn't already know, of course. But it's strange. She says he's not getting nervous as the days go by. If anything, he's relaxing."

"So, the clock is ticking, and he's happy you're not finding whatever it is he doesn't want you to find."

"Exactly. I gotta figure there's something else in the financial records. Maybe McQueen stole more money than we realized. So, is Calloway worried we'll go for a higher judgment?"

"McQueen's guilty. You've got him dead to rights on paper. And we'll be twenty years getting a three-hundred-thousand dollar settlement out of him. Going for a higher judgment doesn't even make sense."

Dallas thanked the waiter as the man set the drinks down on the polished wood bar. "I hate things that don't make sense."

"Me, too."

"Shelby's been looking through the evidence boxes all week."

"*Shelby?*"

"Yeah. I've also got the accounting team going through the computer system."

"You have our receptionist doing financial research?"

"She's very enthusiastic. And she's very bright."

"Ah." Greg nodded. "*Bright* and *enthusiastic*. So that's what they call it these days."

"Get your mind out of the gutter. She's in my office doing research, nothing else. I don't care what Margaret told you."

"In your *office?*"

"It made the most sense."

"Oh, man. You are so far gone over her."

Dallas wasn't about to deny it. Didn't mean he could do anything about it. Didn't mean it was coloring his judgment. "Do you blame me?"

Greg shrugged and took a drink. Canned classical music faded to the background as conversation from the growing predinner crowd grew louder. "I guess if you can't have Allison..."

"You know I think of Allison as a sister."

Greg chuckled. "Have I apologized for nearly taking your head off?"

"No need."

"I wasn't thinking straight. Even if you were screwing around with my fiancée, why would you send me pictures?"

"That would be pretty stupid," Dallas agreed.

"I didn't stop to sort through the logic," said Greg.

"Bad thing for a lawyer."

"That's the problem with women."

"They mess with your logic."

When the waiter signaled for another drink, Dallas nodded. "Take me and Shelby," he said. "There's no logic in me being attracted to her. She's not my type. I don't even know what it is that gets to me."

"Animal lust."

Well, sure. Dallas already knew that much. But it was

more than just animal lust. He'd gone shopping for her at the housewares department for God's sake.

"Must be the lust," he said to Greg.

Greg clapped him on the shoulder. "Take it from me. Get it out of your system and carry on."

Dallas had tried that. Not only hadn't it worked, it had made things worse. "You expect me to take advice from a guy who nearly lost his fiancée last week?"

"She's marrying me next week."

Dallas held up his glass in a toast. "That she is. Congratulations."

Just then, Allison appeared, slipping her arm beneath Greg's and snuggling up next to him. "What are you guys talking about?"

"The Perth-Abercrombie case," Greg answered easily.

"Yawn," said Allison, hopping up on a stool.

Dallas quickly stood up and moved one place down so that Shelby could sit between him and Greg.

She smiled her thanks, and he felt a buzz.

"Find a dress?" Greg asked Allison.

"Sure did. Got one for Shelby, too."

"Going to shock the congregation?" Dallas teased Shelby under his breath. Taking in her black velvet pants and the purple, corset-look blouse that was laced up the front, he wondered if she'd agree to have sex with him on the bar in say, ten seconds.

She leaned toward him. "You'll like this one. It's classy and conservative."

Dallas didn't doubt for a second he'd like it. Shelby could wear a burlap sack and he'd like it. In fact, he'd love it. Worship it. Rip it off her with his teeth.

Her bare shoulder brushed against him, and he had

to fight to keep from looping his hands around her slender waist and pulling her into his lap. The woman was definitely a goddess.

"Care for a drink?" he asked, keeping both hands firmly on top of the bar and including Allison in the question.

"What are you guys having?" asked Allison.

"Scotch," Greg answered.

Allison shuddered. "Yuck. I'll take a vodka martini."

"Scotch works for me," said Shelby. "On the rocks."

Greg bent his head to talk to Allison, and Shelby grinned up at Dallas.

His gaze slid to her cleavage as he picked up their private conversation. "You don't know the meaning of the word 'conservative.'"

"You know, you're way funnier than you let on."

"That wasn't a joke."

A waiter appeared at Greg's shoulder. "Mr. Smith? Mr. Williams? Your dinner table is ready." He made a formal arm gesture toward the dinning room. "This way, please."

Allison and Greg followed him.

When Shelby hopped down from the bar stool, Dallas couldn't resist the temptation to put his hand on the small of her back, like he was being a gentleman, assisting her, guiding her. In reality, he was feeling her hot skin through the tight purple satin and fantasizing about her without the velvet pants, without her panties, wearing just the corset blouse, with the laces dangling open.

He gritted his teeth.

"YOU SURE YOU DON'T MIND stopping at the office?" asked Shelby, feeling guilty for making Dallas go out of his way. After dinner, Allison and Greg had headed for Greg's apartment, so Shelby was pretty sure she'd have Allison's place all to herself well into tomorrow. Peace and quiet. Perfect for concentrating on the computer printouts.

"If you're sure you want to work on a Sunday," said Dallas.

Shelby nodded, turning in her seat, letting her gaze rest on his dark profile. "You know how it is when you can feel there's something out there? Shimmering? It's close, but it's just out of reach?"

"That I do." Dallas nodded, then he cleared his throat. "You want some help?"

The offer surprised Shelby. "You'd have time?"

He pulled into his reserved parking spot beneath a towering streetlight at the front of his office building. He killed the engine and opened his door. The smell of rain blew in from the lake as the garden junipers swayed in the midnight breeze.

"I'll make time," he said as he stepped out of the car, pushing the driver's door closed behind him.

Shelby followed suit.

"The accountants aren't getting anywhere," he continued as they rounded the front of his car, "and Friday morning's coming up fast."

Shelby started up the sweeping, concrete staircase that led to the building's main entrance. "You'll be finished in court in time for the wedding?"

Dallas's footsteps clicked behind her. "Should be no problem. You warm enough?"

"I'm fine."

"Want my jacket?"

"We're almost inside."

He passed his electronic key in front of the sensor and the door pinged open. "Just as well. I kind of like your shirt."

She smiled at him as he opened the door. "Yeah?"

"Yeah."

They started across the tiled foyer, their footsteps echoing in the stillness of the night. Frappino's was dark, with only a small light glowing above the coffee machines. A lone security guard gave them a wave from his position behind the counter on the far side of the foyer.

"What?" asked Shelby. "No sarcastic remarks?"

"About what?"

"About what? About my clothes."

"I like them."

"That's it? You just plain like them."

Dallas punched the elevator button. "That's what I said."

The door slid open and she shook her head as she walked inside. "I can't figure you out."

"I'm pretty simple."

"What? An Aries with Mars rising?"

He chuckled. "No. I'm a man watching a beautiful woman."

She tipped her head and squinted at him. "You after something here?"

His eyes smoldered. "You know it."

Her stomach fluttered, and a flush of desire rushed over her skin. The building suddenly felt very quiet and very empty. The elevator motor roared in her ears.

She dropped her voice. "Am I in danger here?"

"Depends on your definition of danger. You say no, and I'll always respect that." He let the thought trail off.

The elevator door glided smoothly open, and they stepped out into the night-lit hall.

"And if I said yes?" she asked bravely.

"Then I'm all over you." He used another key and opened the Turnball, Williams and Smith door.

They walked in, and it clicked shut behind them.

"Dallas?"

"Yeah?" He continued down the hall, while she followed behind.

"What if I said maybe?"

He inserted a key in the door of his own office. "Red flag to a bull, babe."

He opened the door, hit the switch for the overhead light and headed inside. Shelby paused in the doorway, emotions swirling around inside her.

If she said no, he'd respect that. Somehow the knowledge made him sexier. She'd never met a more disciplined man. If she wasn't already lusting after his body, she'd sure start lusting after his principles.

Plain truth was, she wanted him.

All of him.

And she was tired of making them both suffer.

She flicked off the light. "Maybe," she said to his broad back.

He froze.

It seemed like an eternity before he turned. "You serious?"

She blinked, focusing on his face as her eyes adjusted to the glow from the city lights that cascaded through the glass windows. "What do you think?"

A sizzling smile grew on his face, and he cocked his head sideways. "Drop your pants."

Shelby grinned right back, tossing her hair as she sauntered toward him. She stopped only inches away, reaching for his tie, running the raw silk through her fingertips. "We have *got* to do something about this S and M inclination you've got going."

"I don't want to spank you, Shelby."

"Good. 'Cause you're not going to."

His voice dropped to a husky rumble that more than turned her on. "See, I've had this fantasy going all night long..."

A burst of sexual energy bloomed inside her. Her voice turned breathless. "Yeah?"

He nodded, reaching for the ties on her blouse. "Yeah. It involves this shirt, and your skin, and nothing...much...else."

Shelby's breathing sped up as he loosened the ties, and adjusted her blouse over her breasts. Then he reached down and popped the button on her pants, the backs of his knuckles grazing her belly. The slide of the zipper echoed in the silent room. He kept her gaze trapped with the heat of his own.

He placed his warm, broad hands on the waistband of her pants, rolling them down, along with her panties, pushing everything off over her ankles.

Sexual desire crested in her bloodstream. Her skin was sensitized to his touch, her body drank in his scent, his low, mumbled words vibrated through her system.

He put his hands on her waist and turned her toward his desk. "Hop up," he whispered, lifting her.

Her bottom settled on the cool, polished surface.

"Lean back on your elbows," he coaxed.

A hint of nerves broke through the haze of arousal. "You don't have a Polaroid in here, do you? Just because Allison—"

"No Polaroid." He tapped a finger against the corner of his eye. "Just these."

She slowly leaned back.

He smoothed her hair and pushed her knees slightly apart. Then he stepped away, drinking in the sight of her, his dark eyes smoldering with obvious hunger.

Goose bumps rose on her body. Fingers of sensation worked their way along her skin, as if he was touching her and not just staring. She'd never felt so flat-out desirable in her life.

After a long minute, he spoke in a hoarse whisper. "I don't care what Greg's got in that envelope. This is going to last me the rest of my life."

Shelby waited for him to step forward, *willed* him to step forward. The waiting was exquisite agony and she bit down on her bottom lip, desperately holding back a moan. She wasn't going to beg.

She saw his fists clench by his sides, and his own jaw tightened while they stared at each other in some kind of erotic standoff.

"Shelby," he finally ground out.

"What?" she groaned.

"You haven't said yes."

She closed her eyes and collapsed back, her hot skin contracting against the cold wood. "Yes," she nearly shouted.

He was there in an instant, bending over, his firm lips on hers, his mouth open, his hands stroking, fingers seeking, while her entire body convulsed into a quivering mass of need.

He shucked his clothes, and she frantically kissed his skin, stroked him, grasped him, pressed herself tight against him.

His telephone flew off the desk, along with file folders, business cards and a marble pen holder.

Naked, he rolled on top of her, tangling his hands in her hair, pressing her tight against the hard desktop, his hot flesh counterpoint to the cold wood. He kissed her deeply, pushed aside her blouse, cupped her breasts, circled her nipple, grazed her skin, pulling her closer and tighter against his body.

She couldn't get close enough, couldn't kiss deep enough, wanted to touch every inch of him all at the same time. After long, frantic minutes, he slowed his caresses. She stilled. Their rasping breaths synchronized, and they stared at each other in amazement as he pushed inside.

She felt her eyes flutter closed as sensation overwhelmed her. "Dallassssss..."

"You're incredible." He kissed her once. Then again. Then harder. He opened his mouth and his tongue sought the tender, sensitive places inside her.

Tension coiled and grew and expanded, until she thought she couldn't stand it another second. She gripped the edges of the desk, arching toward him, urging him on, faster and harder, desperate for the feeling to burst, desperate for it to go on forever.

Sweat glistened between them. Dallas's breathing grew deep and guttural. "Tell me... When..."

"Never," she cried. "Always." She hung on.

"Now!" The word was torn from her lips.

Dallas groaned and his body convulsed. A sunburst bloomed on the insides of her eyelids. Heat shot through her, then their sweat turned to cool rain as the world slowly righted itself and the storm subsided.

The first thing she became aware of was Dallas's heavy breathing. She savored the weight of his body. Felt his lungs push against her chest with every breath.

She inhaled his essence, tasted his salty skin, savored his heat between her thighs, and tightened her arms around him for a long, last shudder of ecstasy before reality crowded in.

"You do realize..." She pushed some wayward strands of her hair from where they tickled her eyelashes. "We're officially having an affair."

"I know," he agreed, not making any move to get off her. "But we have six more times before it turns into a relationship."

Shelby pulled her head to one side so she could look at him. "I like the way you think, Williams."

He grinned, still hugging her, still locked together, legs still entwined. "I like the way you feel, Jacobs."

Shelby felt sexy all over again. "We should probably ration them."

"The six times?"

"Yeah."

He drew in a deep breath. "You're right. Like, once a week?"

She'd been thinking once a day, but she agreed with him anyway. Then she shifted, and the stirrings of new desire strummed their way along her thighs.

He pushed her hair back from her forehead and kissed her swollen lips. Then he kissed her eyelids, and her forehead, and her cheeks. Then he went back to her lips. "As long as we don't let go of each other, it's still once, right?"

She twined her arms around his neck. "I *really* like the way you think."

12

SHELBY HAD BEEN staring at the computer printouts for over an hour when there was a knock on Allison's door. She clambered up off the carpet, stepping carefully between the stacks of paper as she dusted off the back of her khaki cargo pants and padded barefoot to the door.

She opened it to find Dallas, looking sexy and rugged in a pair of blue jeans, a dusty-blue T-shirt and a pair of sneakers. He carried a paper coffee cup in each hand. He hadn't shaved, and his tanned skin creased slightly at the corners of his eyes as he smiled.

"Hey," he said, with a tiny nod.

"Hey," she answered, fighting the surge of joy that bubbled up at the sight of him. It was an affair, she reminded herself. A fleeting, temporary affair that might well ruin her life. She shouldn't be so damn happy about it.

"Sleep well?" he asked.

She nodded. "You?"

"The best."

"Yeah?" She realized she wanted a compliment. Some kind of acknowledgment that making love with her had helped him sleep, that maybe she'd had the same emotional effect on him as he was having on her.

"Yeah," he answered simply.

Not quite what she was hoping for, but it looked liked that was all she was going to get. Well, at least he was here, and he'd brought coffee. She glanced down at the cups.

"Mochaccino?" he asked, holding out one of the cups.

"I think I'm in love," she sighed.

Something flinched in his eyes, and she quickly scooped the cup and stepped out of the way. She hadn't meant that the way it sounded, of course. But trying to take it back would only make things worse.

She turned to walk into the living room. "Go ahead and dive right in."

She gestured to the papers on the couch, rattling on to cover for her inappropriate word choice. "On those ones, I've confirmed McQueen did steal money." Then she gestured to the piles in front of the television. "On those ones I've confirmed he didn't. And the ones in the middle haven't been checked."

She plunked herself down on the carpet again, leaning back against Allison's plaid couch as she peeled back the plastic lid of the mochaccino. "If he stole any more money than the accountants first identified, I can't find it.

"I cross-referenced each of the transactions to the computer disk the accountants gave me," she continued. "Everything checks out from timing, to profit, to commission. I've even confirmed that all the companies he dealt with were legit."

Dallas sat down in one of Allison's armchairs. "You ever had accounting training?"

She blinked at him. "Me?"

"I thought you were a cocktail waitress."

"I'm a *legal receptionist*," she corrected. And she sure hoped she got to stay as one after this affair was over.

He leaned forward and picked up a sheaf of paper. "And one hell of a researcher."

"Does that mean you're not going to fire me?"

He glanced up. "Why would I fire you?"

"When this ends—"

"The case?"

"The affair," she scoffed.

He tossed the reports back down, his expression turning serious. "Our personal relationship has no bearing on your standing at the firm."

Shelby wanted to believe him. "You say that now."

"Shelby. I'm a lawyer. If I fire you because you slept with me, thought about sleeping with me, or stopped sleeping with me, I'd be breaking the law."

"And you won't break the law." Why wasn't that much of a comfort to her?

"I won't break the law. And even if there wasn't a law to break, my honor and principles wouldn't allow me to fire you."

Honor and principles. What a novel concept. Neil hadn't had honor and principles. Gerry Bonnaducci sure hadn't had honor and principles.

Maybe she *was* safe with Dallas. Maybe she could let her guard down and simply enjoy his company while they made love six more times, and then got out before things got really complicated.

Six times. She sighed.

It sure didn't seem like much.

"Something wrong?"

She forced a smile. "No. Nothing." Then she glanced around at the scattered papers. "Well, except that we haven't figured out what Randy Calloway knows that we don't know."

Dallas slid off the chair and joined her on the floor, plunking a huge stack of paper into his lap. "Then let's get going."

DALLAS AND SHELBY worked all day, looking for a needle in a haystack—a needle that might not even exist. He had to admit, he admired her focus and concentration as she ploughed through printout after printout. He, on the other hand, kept glancing at the clock, counting down the hours and minutes until midnight, when he could claim it was Monday morning and the start of a whole new week.

They'd agreed to make love once a week, and Dallas didn't see any reason why they had to wait until the end of it. Maybe he'd take her back to his apartment. If they made love until neither of them could walk, then slept in each other's arms, maybe it would be enough to hold him for the next seven days.

Maybe.

He let his gaze shift from the report he was reading over to her once again. A page slipped through his fingers to the floor.

Her head was bent. Strands of her auburn hair had worked free from her ponytail and curled around her cheeks. Her lips were pursed in a moue of concentration, and her cheeks were slightly flushed.

She wore a pair of loose khaki pants, with bare feet, her toes curling and uncurling in the carpet as she worked her way through the lines of numbers. Unless he was mistaken, she wasn't wearing a bra under that mustard-colored tank top.

He felt a hum of arousal growing in the pit of his stomach. He glanced at the clock on the wall. Four-thirty. If he didn't get out of here, he wasn't going to make midnight.

"You hungry?" he asked, levering into a standing position.

She glanced up as if he'd startled her, green eyes blinking. "Hmm?"

"Hungry?" he repeated. "I was going to go get us some pizza."

She shook herself. "Sure. Pizza sounds great."

"Something to go with it? Margaritas?" Maybe the crushed ice would cool him down a little.

She unfolded her legs from beneath her. "You want some money?"

Dallas felt himself bristle. "Don't be ridiculous."

She stood and stretched, showing off her sexy navel. He was growing partial to that little gold ring.

"It's an affair, Dallas," she said. "We should each pay our own way."

He planted his tongue firmly in his cheek. "Why would you start now?"

"Ooo." She pursed her mouth and scrunched up her eyes. "Low blow."

"If we're talking the value of my bottom line," he teased, the tension easing its way out of his gut, "I figure you're up a couple of world cruises."

Her eyes danced like jewels. "I was that good?"

"You were that good."

"You do know this conversation smacks of prostitution."

"You do know that's about a hundred-and-eighty degrees away from how I feel about you."

It took her a second to answer, her eye color inching to turquoise. "That's nice."

It *was* nice. It was also unnerving and confusing. He lusted after her, but he liked her. He respected her intelligence and he cared about her. He'd never coped with a combination of feelings like this before.

It was on the tip of his tongue to tell her so, and to ask her how she felt about him. Was this just a lark? Did she feel like there was a friendship building between them? Did she respect him? Think he was funny? Want to be with him?

A shot of insecurity suddenly hit his system—like that moment before a big trial started, when he knew his case was full of holes.

"What do you want on the pizza?" he asked, putting the relationship analysis firmly on hold.

She shrugged her slim shoulders. "Whatever."

"The works?"

"Sounds great."

"Lime margaritas?"

"They might make the numbers go fuzzy."

"A couple more hours of this, and the numbers will go fuzzy anyway."

"You do have a point."

He winked at her as he headed for the door. "Back in a while."

She smiled and blew him a kiss, and suddenly all was right with his world.

AFTER DALLAS LEFT, Shelby slit open one of the boxes she'd discovered in the Turnball, Williams and Smith storage locker. Dallas had told her the accountants had stopped looking through the dozens of boxes once they had enough evidence on McQueen.

She flipped her way through the first report, surprised to find names of brokers she hadn't come across before. With a sigh of resignation, she pulled her calculator closer and punched her way through the formula she could now do in her sleep.

Click, click, click, confirmed.

Click, click, click, confirmed.

Then, on the third broker's name, she sat up straight. A shot of excitement hit her square in the chest. She rechecked the calculation, and the feeling grew.

She tested another number and another and another. She dropped the report on the floor in front of her, one hand going for her forehead, reflexively pushing her hair back.

She grabbed another report from the new box, and did a bunch of random tests. Johnson, Larkin and Platt. She grabbed another stack of reports from a different time period.

Johnson, Larkin and Platt again. The same three brokers had numerous rounding errors. Nobody else had a single one.

She glanced at the phone, wondering if Dallas had his cell with him, wishing she knew the number. She wanted to tell him *now*. Wanted to scream from the rooftop that she'd found something significant.

Johnson, Larkin and Platt, plus McQueen. Was it an embezzlement ring? What did they have in common? Were there others?

While she waited for Dallas to get back, she tried some more test calculations. Same results, time period after time period. Just the four of them, nobody else.

She headed for the computer, inserted a human resources disk and searched through the records for each man. Larkin was hired in 1998, Platt six months later, then Johnson and McQueen six months after that.

Shelby went back to the earliest financial record.

They'd all been at it for years. Could they have known each other prior to starting at Perth-Abercrombie?

She checked the human resources records again. They'd gone to different universities, had previous jobs in different parts of the country. In fact, the only link she could find between them was that Calvin Abercrombie had hired them all—hardly compelling evidence of a conspiracy.

But how could it be that four different brokers all decided to embark on the same scam at the same time? They had to have at least discussed it.

On a hunch, she called up the employment records of Seth Bendel. He was a computer programmer suspected of helping McQueen, but there wasn't enough evidence to connect him.

Turned out Bendel was hired at the same time as Larkin, and he was also hired by Calvin Abercrombie.

Calvin Abercrombie.

Even speculating about a plot that went that high in the organization sent a shiver down her spine. She told herself she was getting carried away. Of *course* Abercrombie would hire employees. There wasn't any reason in the world to suspect his hiring of these five people was in any way connected to their later crimes.

Still, Shelby checked further into the human resources records.

In the end, Abercrombie had only ever hired eight employees. Two were his personal secretaries, one was a broker who'd only stayed a month, and the other five may have been criminals. It seemed like everyone else in the firm had been hired by the human resources manager.

Shelby's heart began beating faster, and her stomach started to cramp.

She checked on Eamon Perth's hiring record, just for comparison.

He'd only ever hired one employee. His personal secretary.

Shelby sat back in her chair, blinking at the computer screen, feeling suddenly exhausted.

The front door opened and Dallas walked in, balancing a large pizza and a freezer pack of margarita mix.

She turned to stare at him.

"What?" he asked, taking in her face, his expression turning worried.

"I found it."

He plunked the pizza and the mix down on a table. "Found what?"

"What Randy Calloway didn't want us to know."

Dallas's eyes grew wider as he strode over to the computer.

"It was in the unopened boxes. It's Calvin Abercrombie," said Shelby, knowing now that it had to be true. Calvin was somehow connected to the conspiracy.

Dallas's brows knit together. "What about Calvin?"

Shelby gestured to the computer screen, still scrambling to get her head around it. "Abercrombie is behind the thefts."

Dallas stopped short. *"What?"*

"There were four brokers involved, maybe five, maybe the computer programmer, too."

"Shelby, *what* are you talking about? I wasn't even gone an hour."

"McQueen wasn't the only one skimming money." She picked up a stack of printouts with reams of numbers circled and underlined. "Larkin, Johnson and Platt were doing exactly the same thing, during exactly the same time frame."

Dallas frowned at the marked-up report. "What does that have to do with Abercrombie?"

"He hired them all."

Dallas looked up. "So? He must have hired dozens of people."

Shelby clicked the mouse button, bringing up a new computer screen. "He only ever hired eight—his own personal secretaries, the one broker who's since left and the people involved in the crime. Perth only ever hired one. His own personal secretary."

Her heartbeat deepened, and her breathing grew faster as she realized all over again the magnitude of what she'd discovered.

Dallas stayed silent for a full minute.

"It proves nothing," he finally said, tossing the report on the desk.

"It proves there were at least four criminals, not one."

"Maybe," said Dallas. "But that's irrelevant to our case."

She shot to her feet. "What do you mean, it's irrelevant?"

"This case is against McQueen. I'm not introducing a trail of breadcrumbs that will dilute his crime."

She took a staggering step back. "Dilute his crime..." They'd stumbled across the *truth*.

"I'm being paid to put together evidence against McQueen, not the other three."

"But—"

"And Abercrombie?" Dallas's voice went up, his hand raking through his hair. "You expect me to accuse a principal of the firm that *hired me* of a conspiracy?"

Shelby's frustration level pulsed higher. "Dallas—"

"This is circumstantial evidence at best. It would never even make it into a court of law."

"I'm just saying we should look further—"

"No."

"No?"

Dallas shook his head. "I am not about to go off on a wild-goose chase trying to implicate my own client because he happened to have *hired* people."

He took a couple of steps across the paper-strewn living room. "They'd fire Turnball, Williams and Smith just for asking the question. And do you think any other company in its right mind would hire us after *that?*"

Shelby's frustration turned to anger. "What about the truth?" she nearly shouted. "What about your honor and principles?"

"It's against my principles as both a lawyer and a man to try to implicate my *own client*."

Something inside Shelby died. "So you have honor and principles when they're financially convenient."

"That's ridiculous."

"Is it?" She started to gather up the printouts she'd spent so many hours staring at for the past week. She felt deflated, bruised, betrayed. Dallas was no better than Shuster. "And what about me, Dallas?" Her voice was small.

"What about you? I'm the lawyer, you're the receptionist. You're not coming to court. You don't decide what I use or don't use in a case."

"I thought we were doing something together here."

"We were. We *are*."

"But we'd best not mix up our roles."

"What the hell does that mean?"

"It means you're the lawyer and I'm the receptionist, and when push comes to shove, your much-touted principles and honor don't mean a damn thing."

His brow furrowed. "I'm not following—"

"I'll save you the trouble," she said, plunking a large stack of printouts into his arms. "I quit."

"You *what?*"

"You won't need to fire me when this ends badly. I quit."

"But..." He looked shell-shocked, glancing around the room. "We have pizza, margaritas. It's only seven hours 'till midnight."

Shelby didn't understand his point. In fact, she *really* didn't understand his point.

"It's my own fault," she conceded. "I knew it all along. Bosses and sex don't mix."

Dallas whapped the printouts down on the table. "You can't quit over this. It's *one* case."

"It goes to the core of who you are, Dallas." And it went to the heart of Shelby's judgment about men. She'd let her lust for Dallas cloud her judgment. In the end, maybe she *had* wanted sex more than she'd wanted the job.

"Give me a break," said Dallas. "I'd be an unethical lawyer if I *did* try to hang my own client."

"How can you work for a man who'd steal from his own company?"

"We don't know he stole anything."

"And *we* don't want to find out, do we?"

"*We* want to do the job we were hired to do."

Shelby's emotions went flat. "I don't know why I thought I'd be safe with you."

"You *are* safe with me."

She let out a dry laugh. "Only until I get between you and your money. That's what it's about, isn't it? Perth-Abercrombie is a big, important client, and you don't want to lose their business."

He closed his eyes and clenched his jaw. "This is ridiculous."

"Dallas, the last two men I worked for betrayed me because they lacked moral fiber. I thought you were different. I was wrong."

"Shelby, until you pass the bar exam, I suggest you reserve judgment on my moral fiber in this instance."

"I don't need to be a lawyer to understand morality. You're no better than Shuster."

Anger flared in his eyes. "Shuster was out to hang you. I'd protect you. Always."

"Yeah," she scoffed. "As long as I was paying you. And then you'd protect me even if I was a criminal."

"When I met you, you *were* a criminal."

"I was innocent."

He took a step closer to her, obviously warming up to his arguments. "I didn't know that at the time. But I was your lawyer and it was my job to look out for your best interests. Now I'm Calvin Abercrombie's lawyer—"

"It's not the same thing."

"It's exactly the same thing."

"I'm asking you to find out the truth."

"You're asking me to betray my client."

Shelby shook her head and took a couple of steps back. "I may not be a lawyer, but I know that justice is about the truth. You're turning a blind eye and making excuses to protect your business."

"I'm making decisions that are within the law."

"Then the law is at odds with morality."

"I don't want to lose you, Shelby."

"I wasn't that great a receptionist anyway."

"That's not what I meant."

"The affair was almost over."

That seemed to take him aback. "Almost over...?"

"You know what we're like, Dallas. We'd have come up with an excuse to make love every day this week."

Something flared behind his eyes.

"We'd have squandered our six times, and that would be the end of it."

"Shelby—"

"You should leave."

"I can't."

"Goodbye, Dallas." She marched across the room and flung open the door.

"Shelby."

"Go." She closed her eyes so she didn't have to watch him leave, an excruciating pain knifing its way through her chest.

GREG CLICKED Dallas's office door closed behind him on Monday morning. "What? I can't leave you alone with Shelby for five minutes."

Dallas tossed his pen down on the desk. "She decided she didn't like the way we do business."

He still bristled from having his ethics challenged by his receptionist. Who the hell did she think she was?

Bad enough that his father insisted on muddying the waters with tangential, ethical issues at every freaking turn.

The law was the law was the law. That's why they called it the law. That's why they'd gone to so much trouble to write it down, discuss it, challenge it and set precedents on it.

It was his legal right, his legal *obligation* to protect his client's interests. It wasn't his job to persecute the very people who were paying him.

"She told me what happened," said Greg.

"I'm sure she did."

"She was pretty upset."

Dallas stood up. He was pretty damned upset, too. "If the woman refuses to understand my perspective, I'm better off without her."

"Don't you mean *we're* better off without her?"

"That's what I said."

"No. You said *I*." Greg took a few steps into the office and dropped into a guest chair. "Is this about more than just the case?"

Dallas snarled, dropping back down into his chair. "Apparently it's about my entire character and worth as a human being."

"What went on between the two of you?"

"We had sex," said Dallas. Though he inwardly recoiled at the crude term, he kept his face poker-straight.

"Nothing more?"

"Nothing more." And that was the truth. There hadn't been time for anything more. They'd been hot for each other's bodies, and that was it.

"No sticky emotional involvement?"

"We're talking about Shelby here. How far away from my type can you get?"

Greg cocked his head. "We call you the Iceman behind your back, you know."

Dallas didn't understand the relevance of that remark, so he waited for Greg to explain.

"I've never seen you this upset before. Not about work, not about a woman, not about anything." Then a light suddenly dawned behind Greg's eyes, his expression turning triumphant. "Except..." He pointed a finger in the air.

A sinking feeling formed in the pit of Dallas's stomach. "What?"

"Except when you argue with your father."

Dallas threw up his hands. "Exactly. Shelby uses the same underhanded techniques as he did."

Greg paused. "Dallas, your father is a top litigator with thirty years' experience. You mean to tell me Shelby can hold a candle to him?"

"Not that way. It's the morality question, the your-principles-have-to-be-my-principles attitude—"

"Or maybe it's the fact that you love them both."

Dallas felt as though the floor had dropped right out from under him. He opened his mouth to rebut, but no sound came out.

"Come on, Dallas. You can't even see straight around the woman. You think the entire world is lusting after her. You've moved her into your office. You're sleeping with her. You let her get under your skin in a way that's reserved for your family alone. Wake up and smell the mochaccino."

Dallas found his voice. "You're insane."

Greg grinned broadly, like a man who'd just delivered the coup de grace in a supreme sourt proceeding. "Been there. Done that. Know what I'm talking about."

"I am not, repeat *not* in love with Shelby Jacobs." Greg had gone off the deep end on this one. The woman couldn't even pick out a decent dress. They had nothing in common but mutual lust. Her aspirations were not his aspirations. Her values were not his values.

"You sure about that?" asked Greg quietly.

"I'm positive about that. You're five days away from your wedding, and I think you have hearts and flowers on the brain."

Greg stared at him in quizzical silence.

"If you don't mind, I've got a case to win on Friday," said Dallas.

Greg stood up. "Then I'll get out of your way."

EARLY WEDNESDAY MORNING, Shelby sat in the silence of Allison's kitchen circling potential employment ads. The café waitress job was still up for grabs, though the evening janitorial openings were now limited.

She heard the shower shut off upstairs and the kettle whistle shrilly on the countertop. She stood up to make tea so that it would be ready when Allison got downstairs. Hopefully, breakfast would be over quickly. For some bizarre reason, this was the hardest time of the day.

Getting up with Allison, eating bagels, drinking tea and getting an early start to their respective, real, dignified jobs, had made her feel like a winner. She'd loved it at Turnball, Williams and Smith.

Her chest tightened, and she closed her eyes, gripping the lip of the countertop. She never should have slept with Dallas. If she hadn't slept with him, maybe she wouldn't have felt so personally affronted by his decision on the Perth-Abercrombie case.

As a group, lawyers were hardly the most honorable people in the world. And she'd sure never given a second thought to the decisions Greg or Allan made on their cases. She hadn't even known what their cases were. Didn't expect to know what they were. Didn't want to know what they were.

The problem started because she'd crossed the line with Dallas. A line she'd known was there. A line she'd known she wasn't supposed to cross. It was all her own fault.

A single tear slipped between her lashes.

She was never going to get a proper job. Never going to have a successful life. Never going to argue with Dallas, joke with Dallas, laugh with Dallas again.

Another tear slipped through.

She was never going to lie in his arms in the early morning light, holding her breath so a new day wouldn't start and separate them.

She inhaled on a shudder, and her fingertips went to her mouth. It was all mixed up. Her job, her affair with Dallas, her emotions...

"Shelby?" Allison touched her shoulder.

Her voice trembled. "I'm fine."

Allison put an arm around her shoulders and squeezed. "No, you're not."

Shelby gave a jerky nod. "It's no big deal."

"Go back to the job. They haven't filled it."

"I can't."

"Why not? Dallas will be professional. It'll all blow over."

Shelby tried to imagine herself in the receptionist

desk, with Dallas a few steps down the hall. Ironically, it wasn't the thought of his legal ethics that bothered her, it was the knowledge that, in her heart, the affair had turned into a relationship.

Looking back, she didn't blame him for being so angry. She was his receptionist, his good-time girl. She had no business judging his morals and principles, expecting that he'd care about her opinion. It wasn't a relationship on his side, but somehow she'd turned it into one on her side.

She'd been wrong.

She'd fallen fast and hard for Dallas. And she couldn't go into an office on a Monday morning and turn that off.

"Hey." Allison squeezed tight, and Shelby realized there were tears running down her face.

"I'm fine," she repeated, wiping them away. "Just a little bit tired."

"What happened between the two of you?"

Shelby shrugged. "I told you. We slept together. We argued. We joked. We fought. And I quit."

"I mean, emotionally."

Shelby shrugged again. "That was it."

Allison pulled back to look Shelby in the eyes. "You didn't fall for him."

"What's to fall? He's staid, conservative and judgmental." Maybe if she told herself that often enough, she'd believe it.

"But not in bed."

Despite herself, Shelby felt a warm glow invade the pit of her stomach. She gave a watery chuckle. "No, not in bed." And sometimes not out of bed, either. Sometimes he was downright outrageous, and sometimes he was downright fun.

"Do you miss him?" Allison whispered.

Yes. Oh, God, *yes!* "I miss my paycheck."

Allison patted her shoulder. "Then we'd better find you a new job."

13

DALLAS ENTERED the courtroom on Friday morning, knowing the case was going to be a slam dunk. They had everything they needed to get a judgment against McQueen. Both Perth and Abercrombie were in the gallery watching, and they were going to see a capable, professional lawyer at work—a capable, professional lawyer they'd have no qualms about putting on retainer.

Dallas had banished both his father's and Shelby's voices from his brain last night. All of his self-doubts were put to rest, and he was carrying on in the best interest of his client. By the time the day was done, he'd have the Perth-Abercrombie account in the bag, and Greg could go on his honeymoon knowing they'd be able to leverage the win into a contract with Preston International.

Turnball, Williams and Smith were all but launched.

The judge entered the courtroom and the bailiff instructed the court to come to order. "The Honorable Judge Laurent presiding."

The judge sat down. "Be seated," she said, shuffling a few of the papers on the bench in front of her. "Okay, let's hear from the plaintiff."

Dallas stood. "Your Honor. We intend to prove that the defendant, Ralph McQueen, embezzled over three-hundred-thousand dollars from the firm of Perth-

Abercrombie since he was hired as a broker in 1999. We have audited accounting records showing that commissions were miscalculated, that funds were funneled to the annual bonus checks for Mr. McQueen, and that subsequent deposits were made to his personal bank account.

"Mr. McQueen planned the crime, executed the crime, and reaped the profits of the crime, costing Perth-Abercrombie shareholders thousands of dollars and damaging the reputation of the firm."

The judge turned her attention to Randy Calloway. "The defense?" she asked.

Randy Calloway stood on his feet. "Your Honor, my client had no knowledge of the embezzled funds. He is not a computer programmer, and had nothing to do with the development of the software which made the error. Further, there is no proof he thought his bonus checks were any different that those of his fellow employees. He neither printed nor issued nor signed those checks. My client is innocent."

Randy sat down, and it was Dallas's turn to call his first witness.

As the arguments progressed, the witnesses gave testimony and the evidence was introduced, it became obvious to everyone that Dallas was going to win. They had Ralph McQueen dead to rights, and his protestations of ignorance were not swaying the judge.

Randy Calloway was providing a competent defense, though definitely not a stellar one. At first Dallas thought Calloway was simply a mediocre lawyer, and McQueen hadn't wanted to spend a whole lot of money on a lost cause.

But it was more than strange that Calloway hadn't

said word one about the other potential culprits. He *had* to know about them. Why else had he been grilling Shelby every day?

If McQueen was Dallas's client, he'd be bringing up the others at every opportunity, even if the judge would throw it out.

It was almost as if...

Dallas glanced from Calloway's expression to Abercrombie's and back again. If Dallas was a conspiracy theorist he'd think Calloway was more interested in protecting the embezzlement ring than in protecting his own client.

He stilled.

What if Calloway was protecting Abercrombie?

As soon as it formed, Dallas shook that speculation right out of his head. He was Abercrombie and Perth's attorney, not McQueen's. This hearing had two sides, one going after McQueen and one protecting him. Dallas was going after him.

Defense was his father's specialty.

Still, he couldn't help another glance at Abercrombie. Did the man look smug?

Hell, even if he did look smug, it was probably because he was winning the case. *Dallas* was winning the case. Which was exactly what he needed to concentrate on doing.

The middle of a court case was not the place for a mental debate on the ethics of truth and justice. He'd had a thousand of those in law school, a thousand of them with his father. He was here to represent his client's interest, and that was that.

He sure wished Shelby's voice would get the hell out of his head. *I may not be a lawyer, but I know that justice is about the truth. You're turning a blind eye and making excuses to protect your business.*

Was he turning a blind eye?

Dallas's breathing rate increased. What if Abercrombie *was* guilty? What if Perth knew? What if they were hanging McQueen out to dry to protect themselves? If they'd bought both the prosecution and the defense, then the truth had been trampled beneath money and power.

Dallas snapped his head up as he realized he was mentally quoting his father. When the shock of that wore off, he realized he had about ten seconds to choose between his career and his father and Shelby's principles.

The judge was about to call for closing arguments.

Dallas scrambled to make the right choice. If Abercrombie was guilty, he could prove it here and now. But the hit to his career would be enormous. Worse, if Dallas publicly accused Abercrombie, and the man turned out to be *innocent*, Dallas would be chasing ambulances in Mudville.

He weighed the merits of protecting his own financial future. After all, he didn't *know* Abercrombie was guilty. All he had to do was stick to the game plan for ten more minutes and he was home free.

Then he weighed the merits of Shelby's passion on truth and justice, and everything his father had ever tried to teach him. For the first time in his life, he thought he understood his father's fervor. Didn't mean he wanted to become an impoverished zealot, but he did understand the overwhelming emotional urge to fight injustice, even at a personal cost.

It was powerful.

It was seductive.

He stood up.

The judge looked at him quizzically. "Yes, Mr. Williams?"

"I'd like to call Calvin Abercrombie to the stand."

There was a quick buzz of conversation before the judge brought her gavel down. "Very well. Mr. Abercrombie."

Dallas stared down at the table, ostensibly organizing his notes while Calvin made his way to the stand. He tried to shake the knowledge that this might be the stupidest move he'd ever made. No matter which way it went, he'd have to dissolve his partnership with Greg and Allan. No corporation in the world would trust themselves to Dallas ever again.

Maybe he'd open a private practice.

He chuckled coldly to himself. He had a fair amount of money in his savings account. He wouldn't have the lifestyle he'd planned, of course. But he supposed, in the end, you couldn't fight genetics.

Looked like he was going down in a blaze of glory. He squared his shoulders and stared Calvin Abercrombie straight in the eyes. "Were you instrumental in the hiring of three brokers named Johnson, Larkin and Platt?"

Abercrombie's face wrinkled into a mask of rage. His hands tightened on the arms of the chair and, for a second, Dallas thought he might come right out of the witness stand.

"The witness will answer the question," said the judge.

"I was instrumental in the hiring of many people," Abercrombie ground out.

"I'm talking about these three, specifically," said Dallas.

"I don't remember."

"Are you aware that they were embezzling money from Perth-Abercrombie at the same time and in the same manner as Mr. McQueen?"

There was a sudden buzz of conversation in the courtroom. Dallas didn't dare turn around. While he'd never been crazy about Abercrombie, he liked and respected Eamon Perth. And he'd just betrayed the man's trust.

The judge's gavel came down again and the room turned silent.

"No, I was not," Abercrombie lied.

Dallas could feel pinpoints of sweat forming beneath his suit. Not a good sign. He realized at that moment that he hadn't fully considered the price of *not* proving Abercrombie guilty.

"You are saying," Dallas continued, "under oath, under penalty of perjury, that four brokers which you personally hired—and I have the human resources records to prove that they were the only staff members you ever hired except for your personal secretaries and one employee who had left the firm—were involved in a conspiracy to defraud the company and you knew nothing about it?"

Abercrombie hesitated. His gaze shifted to the left for a split second, and the confidence left his tone. "No."

"No, you're not saying that. Or, no, you knew nothing about the conspiracy?"

"No. I knew nothing about any conspiracy."

Dallas took a stab in the dark. "Would you change your answer if I introduced personal checks from the four brokers to you? Called witnesses that put the four of you together?"

Calloway jumped to his feet. "I object."

The judged blinked at Calloway. "When did Mr. Abercrombie become your client?"

Calloway blanched as he realized his error.

The judge turned her attention to Dallas. "Mr. Williams, I caution you that Mr. Abercrombie is not on trial here."

"I understand, Your Honor."

"In light of that fact, I will ask the witness to step down..."

Dallas saw his entire law career flash before his eyes, crashing and burning in this moment, this exact second.

But then the judge continued. "...and I will call for closing arguments in the case of Mr. McQueen. However, I am also recommending Mr. Abercrombie be tried for fraud, conspiracy and embezzlement."

Dallas nearly staggered as a great weight came off his shoulders.

He sailed through his closing arguments. He knew he should be upset about blowing his corporate law career, but he wasn't. The expression on Abercrombie's face when the judge decided to bring him to trial was worth ten corporate law careers.

He understood now that his dad was a justice junkie. He didn't care about the money, he went for the rush. Not that Dallas had stopped caring about the money. He was still going for a career that paid the bills, though maybe not to the exclusion of the rush.

Calloway finished his closing arguments and the judge found for the plaintiff in the amount of three-hundred-thousand dollars plus court costs. Dallas had won.

By the time he loaded his briefcase and turned around, most of the spectators, including Eamon Perth, had left the courtroom. Just as well.

There was only one lone man still sitting in the back row.

Dallas did a double take. "Dad?"

His father stood up.

Dallas hustled down the aisle. "What are you doing here?"

"Greg invited me to the wedding."

"He did?"

Jonathan Williams nodded at his son. "Thought I'd stop here on the way and see you in action."

Dallas didn't know what to say. His brain was a clanging whirlpool of emotion and implications. He'd just blown apart his old life, and he had no idea where the new one was going to lead. At the same time, he was reevaluating everything, including his relationship with his father.

His father smiled. "I have to say, I'm proud of you, son."

The cacophony inside Dallas's head stilled. "You are?"

He father nodded. "That was a gutsy move. You do realize this is going to hit the press."

Dallas hadn't thought of that. He sure hoped the publicity wouldn't hurt Greg and Allan.

His father's nod changed to a shake. "Calvin Abercrombie up on charges of embezzlement? You might want to change your phone number." Then he slapped

Dallas between the shoulder blades. "Or come and stay at my place. Nina wouldn't mind."

"Nina?"

"She and the kids moved in with me."

"They did?"

"We're thinking about getting married."

BY THE END of Allison and Greg's wedding ceremony, Shelby was a basket of nerves. Walking down the aisle was the first time she'd seen Dallas since their fight. He looked gorgeous and sexy and strong, and she could almost feel his arms around her.

She'd kept her face front while the minister spoke and Allison and Greg exchanged vows. She was overjoyed for her friend, but she could feel Dallas's presence sizzling in the background.

Now the organ music swelled and the couple headed back down the aisle. Shelby turned, focusing on Dallas's chest before turning again and taking his arm for the recessional march. The heat of his body seemed to burn into her. The smiling faces of the wedding guests blurred in front of her as memories of Dallas crowded in.

She didn't know how she was going to make it through the evening, or how she'd ever attend a social function with Allison and Greg again, if Dallas was going to be around.

Maybe the town wasn't big enough for the both of them. Maybe she'd have to leave Chicago altogether. She didn't have a new job yet. Maybe this was the time to make a whole new start.

They walked through the church doorway, following close behind Greg and Allison. As they emerged outside, flashbulbs snapped and reporters stuffed microphones in front of their faces.

Wait a minute.

Microphones?

"I am *so* damn sorry," she heard Dallas say to Greg.

"Forget about it," said Greg, hustling Allison into a waiting limo.

Dallas's strong arm went around Shelby's waist and he all but carried her across the sidewalk to the second limo. The shouts of the reporters were a jumble in her mind. She thought she saw a news van with a satellite dish on top.

"What on earth—"

Dallas slammed the door behind her, and hustled around the back of the limo, reporters dogging his every step.

She peered through the tinted windows, feeling like a rock star. Why would the media be interested in Greg and Allison's wedding? Was Greg secretly a European prince or something?

Dallas made it inside the door and wrenched it shut. He reached forward to tap on the glass, signaling the driver to leave. The car inched its way from the front of the church.

Shelby blinked at Dallas. "What was *that* all about?"

"The hearing," said Dallas, straightening his tux.

"The Perth-Abercrombie hearing?"

Dallas nodded.

Shelby turned to stare out the back window at the crowd of reporters in front of the church. They grew smaller as the limo picked up speed.

"I put Abercrombie on the stand," said Dallas.

Shelby whirled her attention back to him. "You *questioned* him?"

"Yeah."

Shelby tried to control the butterflies taking over her stomach. "About Johnson, Larkin and Platt?"

Dallas shrugged. "A retainer from Perth-Abercrombie is out of the question now. And it'll mean dissolving my partnership with Greg. I'm sure sorry about that, but I can't drag him and Allan down with me—"

"What do you mean, drag them down?"

Dallas stared into her eyes. "No corporate entity in the world is going to hire our firm now. I just destroyed the life and the business of one of my own clients." He gave a harsh laugh. "But truth and justice took the day. The judge is issuing an indictment."

"We were right?" asked Shelby, her heart going out to Dallas.

"*You* were right."

"Oh, Dallas." She wanted to put her arms around him and tell him everything was going to be okay. But what did she know? Maybe he'd ruined his own life. Maybe *she'd* ruined his life. "I'm so sorry."

He gave her a crooked smile. "Now, why would you be sorry?"

"You just said—"

"I didn't do it for you, Shelby."

Okay. Now she was embarrassed. "I never thought..."

"I did it because it was the right thing to do. You were right about the honor and principles argument, but it was my decision."

"Of course."

Dallas unexpectedly reached for her hand. He lifted it to his lips and kissed her knuckles.

Shelby felt a jolt of desire, a jolt of sympathy, and a jolt of regret.

"I know our affair is over," he said.

Shelby gripped the edge of the limo seat. She didn't want their affair to be over. They had six more chances to make love, and she wanted them all. It took every ounce of willpower she possessed not to launch herself into his lap and beg him to keep the affair going.

Instead, she nodded.

"Yeah," he sighed, still holding her hand, his thumb absently stroking her palm, ratcheting up her arousal. "And I know we can't do a relationship."

Again Shelby nodded, but inside she wanted to cry. All she wanted was a relationship with Dallas. A long relationship with Dallas. A relationship where she could hold him, laugh with him, fight with him and love him.

Though her body didn't move on the limo seat, her heart quietly cracked in two.

"I know I shouldn't even be thinking about this today," he said. "Since today seems destined to create problems in my life, not solve them." He drew in a long breath. "Do you have any idea how many problems I created at the courthouse?"

Shelby shook her head, afraid to try to speak.

"It boggles the mind. I don't do things like that, you know. I don't leave chaos and destruction in my wake. I don't blow multimillion dollar contracts for my firm."

He put Shelby's hand to his lips again. "And I don't fall in love with wild-and-crazy women who wear sexy dresses and drive me out of my mind."

Shelby's breathing stopped. Her battered heart clunked once against the inside of her chest. Her mouth went dry and sweat burst out on her palms.

"I was thinking," said Dallas.

She tried to speak, but her vocal chords had shut down.

The limo pulled into the circular driveway of the reception hotel, and Shelby could see Allison and Greg emerging under the portcullis.

"Since we blew the one-night stand," Dallas continued. "And we blew the affair. And we don't want a relationship, for a bunch of very, very good reasons." He chuckled to himself, then sobered and stared deeply into Shelby's eyes. "Why don't we skip all the complicated stuff and just get married?"

The limo came to a halt.

Before Shelby could answer, or rather before Shelby could *ask* what on earth Dallas was talking about, a bellman opened the door and reached for her hand.

"Think about it," said Dallas, opening his own door as the bellman helped her out. "I'm going to be here for a few hours."

Marry Dallas? *Marry Dallas?*

Flash bulbs went off in her peripheral vision and reporters yelled questions from behind the hotel staff's barricade, adding to the air of unreality.

Allison appeared and linked her arm through Shelby's. "This way for the *official* wedding pictures."

Since it hardly seemed appropriate to discuss Dallas's proposal during Allison's wedding photographs, Shelby kept her mouth shut. Along with the flower girl and ring bearer, Allison's and Greg's parents joined them in the hotel's small photo studio.

First they took the bride and her attendants, then the groom with his, then the couple and the parents and finally the entire party. Shelby kept half an eye on the proceedings, and half an eye on Dallas as she tried to sift through her shock.

He looked gorgeous in his tux, which was no surprise. As he interacted with those around him, she was reminded that he was intelligent, witty, generous and successful. So, why on earth would he want to marry her?

Sleep with her, okay, yeah. She wasn't stupid, and she'd had plenty of propositions in her time. Maybe she'd misunderstood what he said. How had he phrased it?

Why don't we skip all the complicated stuff and just get married?

Nope. Not much chance she'd misunderstood that. There weren't a whole lot of generally accepted interpretations for the word marriage.

"Ladies' room?" asked Allison, startling Shelby. "Before we go into dinner?"

"Yeah. Sure." Shelby smiled and nodded.

"You holding up okay?" asked Allison as they crossed the lobby to the interested stares of dozens of hotel guests.

"I'm fine," said Shelby, desperately trying to recover her sense of equilibrium. "How about you? Those reporters were wild."

"Can you believe Dallas *did* that? He made the national news."

"He says he'll have to leave the law firm," said Shelby.

Allison waved a hand in dismissal. "Greg's not going to let him do that."

"Won't he drag the firm down?"

"Greg doesn't seem worried. You know what else I can't believe?"

"What?"

Allison raised her eyebrows and gave a crooked frown. "That Greg and I were actually talking business in the limousine between our wedding ceremony and the reception. Doesn't that man ever learn?"

"This does not bode well for the rest of your life," Shelby deadpanned.

"No, it does not," said Allison. "I may need more pictures for his luggage."

Shelby laughed.

"That's the first time I've heard you laugh all week," said Allison.

Shelby sighed, realizing she felt light again. "It is, isn't it?"

Allison nodded. "Are you having a particularly good time at my wedding, or did something happen?"

There was no point in lying. "Dallas proposed."

"He *what*?" Allison shrieked, turning heads in the lobby.

"Proposed," Shelby whispered as they headed into the powder room. "I can't figure it out."

"Did you say yes?" asked Allison.

"I didn't answer. There wasn't time. Why would he propose?"

"Maybe because he's in love with you."

"How could he be in love with me? I'm not classy and sophisticated and intelligent. I have no money. I have no job. What is there? What would attract him?"

"Shelby. Not that I couldn't answer any and all of those questions at length. But you should be having this conversation with Dallas."

"You may have a point." If he did love her. If he *did* love her...

Allison nudged her. "You love him?"

Shelby bit her bottom lip.

"Go on," said Allison with a grin. "You can say it."

"The thought of being with him... Every day, every night, for the rest of my life..."

"Yeah...?" Allison prompted.

"Is so great, I feel like I can't even hold it all."

"You love him," said Allison. "You definitely love him."

"I love him," said Shelby. "I sure hope he was serious."

Allison laughed out loud.

After they left the ladies' room, Shelby practically floated her way across the reception hall. A string orchestra played in one corner, and the room was alive with flowers, balloons, crepe paper and glitter. The guests were chatting over predinner drinks, milling around in the muted light and perfumed air.

She found Dallas near the head table, coming up behind him, desperately wanting to slip her arm through his and feel the heat of his body against her.

"You love me?" she whispered instead.

"Yeah," he replied, reaching down and linking his fingers with hers.

"Why?" she had to ask.

"Beats the hell out of me," he responded with a trace of laughter. "Though it could be because you're gorgeous, funny, intelligent, hardworking and sexy."

"You think?"

"Or maybe it's because you're flip, sarcastic and argumentative."

"Or maybe it's because I'm always right."

"Hadn't thought of that one."

Shelby felt a glow building inside her. "And you want to marry me?"

He leaned down and kissed the top of her head. "That I do."

"If I say no?"

"I walk away. I live forever in abject misery, but I walk away."

"If I say yes?"

She could hear the laughter in his voice. "Then I'm all over you."

"And if I say maybe?"

He snaked his arm around her waist. "Red flag to a bull, babe. I pursue you with everything I've got."

"Which apparently isn't much after today."

"I guess you haven't heard."

"Heard what?"

"Perth's here. He and the other shareholders just turfed Abercrombie and appointed Turnball, Williams and Smith as their permanent counsel. I've got plenty to pursue you with."

"Yeah?"

"Yeah."

She grinned. "Okay then, maybe."

"Perfect," he nodded. "There's a hotel room, roses and champagne all lined up for later."

Shelby moved to rest her cheek against his broad chest. "I love the way you think, Williams."

He enfolded her in a hug, speaking softly against the

top of her head. "And I love everything about you, Jacobs."

She sighed as every little piece of her life settled into perfection. "Me, too."

His heart of stone beat only for her...
Debut author

gena showalter

the Stone Prince

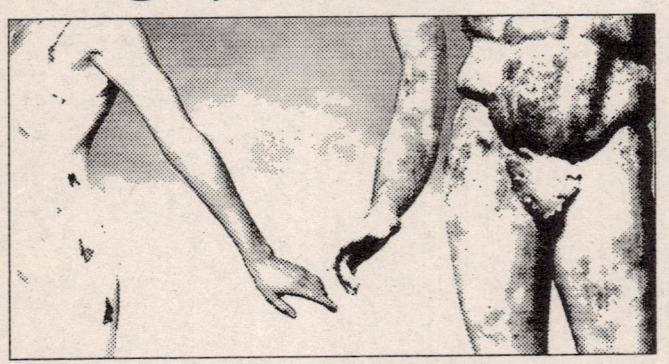

Katie Jones was so unlucky in love that she'd been reduced to kissing the marble statue in her garden. But her luck changed when that so-called statue warmed to life in her arms—and turned out to be a man straight out of any woman's fantasy!

Look for *The Stone Prince* in September.

HQN™
We *are* romance™
www.eHarlequin.com

eHARLEQUIN.com

For **FREE online reading,** visit www.eHarlequin.com now and enjoy:

Online Reads
Read **Daily** and **Weekly** chapters from our Internet-exclusive stories by your favorite authors.

Red-Hot Reads
Turn up the heat with one of our more sensual online stories!

Interactive Novels
Cast your vote to help decide how these stories unfold...then stay tuned!

Quick Reads
For shorter romantic reads, try our collection of Poems, Toasts, & More!

Online Read Library
Miss one of our online reads? Come here to catch up!

Reading Groups
Discuss, share and rave with other community members!

For great reading online, visit www.eHarlequin.com today!

INTONL

Silhouette

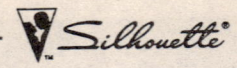

SPECIAL EDITION™

A sweeping new family saga

THE PARKS EMPIRE

Dark secrets. Old lies. New loves.

Twenty-five years ago, Walter Parks got away with murder...or so he thought. But now his children have discovered the truth, and they will do anything to clear the family name—even if it means falling for the enemy!

Don't miss these books from six favorite authors:

ROMANCING THE ENEMY
by Laurie Paige
(Silhouette Special Edition #1621, on sale July 2004)

DIAMONDS AND DECEPTIONS
by Marie Ferrarella
(Silhouette Special Edition #1627, on sale August 2004)

THE RICH MAN'S SON by Judy Duarte
(Silhouette Special Edition #1634, on sale September 2004)

THE PRINCE'S BRIDE by Lois Faye Dyer
(Silhouette Special Edition #1640, on sale October 2004)

THE MARRIAGE ACT by Elissa Ambrose
(Silhouette Special Edition #1646, on sale November 2004)

THE HOMECOMING by Gina Wilkins
(Silhouette Special Edition #1652, on sale December 2004)

Available at your favorite retail outlet.

Visit Silhouette Books at www.eHarlequin.com   SSETPEMINI

eHARLEQUIN.com

Your favorite authors are just a click away at www.eHarlequin.com!

- Take our **Sister Author Quiz** and we'll match you up with the author most like you!

- Choose from over 500 author **profiles!**

- Chat with your favorite authors on our **message boards.**

- Are you an author in the making? Get advice from published authors in **The Inside Scoop!**

- Get the latest on **author appearances** and tours!

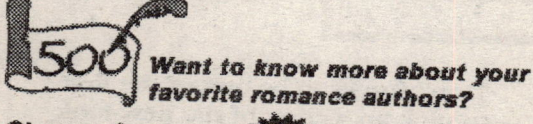

Want to know more about your favorite romance authors?

Choose from over 500 author profiles!

Learn about your favorite authors in a fun, interactive setting— visit www.eHarlequin.com today!

Receive a FREE hardcover book from

HARLEQUIN ROMANCE®

in September!

Harlequin Romance celebrates the launch of the line's new cover design by offering you this exclusive offer valid only in September, only in Harlequin Romance.

To receive your FREE HARDCOVER BOOK written by bestselling author Emilie Richards, send us four proofs of purchase from any September 2004 Harlequin Romance books. Further details and proofs of purchase can be found in all September 2004 Harlequin Romance books.

Must be postmarked no later than October 31.

Don't forget to be one of the first to pick up a copy of the new-look Harlequin Romance novels in September!

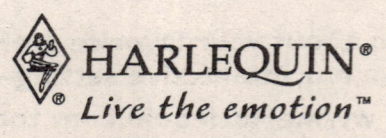

HARLEQUIN®
Live the emotion™

Visit us at www.eHarlequin.com

HRPOP0904